KATHERINE DAHLQUIST-BAUER

MEMORIES OF MY SKIN

Publishing label: ONDALY

ISBN Hardcover: 978-3-903521-05-6

ISBN Softcover: 978-3-903521-04-9

ISBN E-Book: 978-3-903521-10-0

Imprint: ONDALY GmbH

Mariahilfpark 2

6020 Innsbruck

connect@ondaly.com

Cover Art: Ayoola M. Cheakina

Proofreading: Ester Wilson

To Emily and Eleanor, who are infinitely saner than their fictional namesakes.

Emily, thank you for keeping me crazy.

Eleanor, thank you for putting up with my craziness.

Thanks to both of you for letting me use your names.

And to Sydney Doolittle and all of the other shamrocks who loved her. Thanks to all of you, I am who I am today. This book would not have been possible without all of y'all.

Chapter One

S kin yearns, and aches, for memories, and for love.

Seven years had passed since her touch had intertwined with mine, yet still my skin sought hers, soliciting touch from friends who looked like her, kisses from lovers that sounded like her, women whom I spoiled, demanding only darkness until morning came and I found myself breathing beside a woman other than the one of whom I'd dreamt.

As Hélène had put it, I'd been making love to a ghost and having sex with an actress.

Over time, she'd learned never to speak of the woman of whom there was no need to.

The only woman with a right to speak of *her* was far away, and when she called, she never asked. My family, who should have at least pretended they wanted to know how I had been since her death, hadn't spoken with me since.

They couldn't accept the life I led.

I wouldn't accept that they couldn't, not because I loved my lovers, but because I had loved *her* and because I nearly loved Hélène. But I had loved loving Hélène not because of infatuation but because I needed a body beside my own to survive the sleepless nights of a year so miserable and recent it is futile to date, and because dates belong not to my mundane, but to history books and stories or in reference to the day marked on a tombstone as May 12, 2013.

It was seven years since and also the day Hélène left me without warning but with enough time to cry before my annual call from Emily came.

By then, the only remnants of Hélène were half-empty bottles of perfume not permitted on carry-on luggage.

Not even her scent lingered, having been covered by coffee I'd spilled as though to banish her smell before she left without so much as a handshake.

For half a year, I had opened my home to her, never complaining that she couldn't pay bills, that her closeness intruded upon my art, that she never sanitized her hands.

Despite her heavy accent, she possessed precise, dramatic speech sprinkled with monologues prepared for the mediocre plays she hoped to star in.

When she delivered her break-up speech that morning, I shifted between detesting and desiring her false Francophone syllables as she delved into meta-theatrical criticism of my inability to cope with a loss I should have confronted long ago, my refusal to allow anyone to comfort me, my inability to love, not to mention that in the months we'd been together, I failed to pronounce her name properly, adding an "h" I insisted should have been sounded since it was written while refraining from commenting on her subtly incorrect pronunciation of my own name – Kitty and not Kit-ee – while she complained that in the time we'd been together, I'd never once mentioned the woman she claimed possessed me, to which I responded that I was curious as to how she was so intimately familiar with the details of a relationship I'd never mentioned. She refuted by explaining this was the very reason she had to leave.

Because I was lost, and so long as she was with me, so was she.

So, she would return to France where she believed she would be less lost and better loved in the arms of a mother she otherwise did nothing but complain about but whose name brought tears to her eyes as she stood halfway between her departure and the hallway.

I tried to make light of the situation, saying I'd been under the impression that the French preferred fucking without loving, a remark that denied me the *bisous* I'd come to cherish at even the most insignificant greetings and partings. That remark left me alone behind a slammed door in a space I suddenly despised in a city where I no longer wanted to live, seven years from where I wanted to be.

For hours afterward, I sat without crying, without moving except to sip cold coffee until my phone rang, realizing from the thrill that tingled within me that everything Hélène had said was true and that I didn't even resent it despite almost wishing I hadn't hidden my heart from a woman who had done nothing wrong except not being the one I wanted. Almost.

"Darling!"

Even through tiny cell phone speakers, Emily's voice sounded like a song. I forced my tone to sound as pleasant as hers, and as Hélène had often told me, if something was said enough or in the right way, it became true, so my non-negative answer to Emily's inquiry about my state of being was not entirely false, for which I was glad because I couldn't lie to Emily, not even when she was an ocean and a telephone line away.

These talks, though short and scarce, had become more sacred than the insignificant and silent hours spent with my own mother or the many loud and passionate hours passed with lovers.

I was careful, though, never to burden Emily.

It was a day of mourning, and I could only be honored that she chose to spend a sliver of it with me through one end of a speaker.

There was always a period of small talk during which I told her of whatever city and country I was in, of the galleries that grew as every year I was adorned with more of the glamor that accompanies success. I told her everything except of the women who came with it, even though this year there was only one.

If it weren't all but a preface, my conversation with Emily might have been interesting.

I prepared to tell her about Vienna and my upcoming exhibitions, but she hesitated, and I held my breath during her silence, anticipating words similar to those she said every year: that she missed *her* or that she missed me, that she wished things had been different, that her heart was broken, and that she loved me.

With greater tenderness than she'd ever said any of those things, she whispered.

"I want you to come home."

From her tone, I could tell she was not expressing a wistful desire she knew wouldn't be fulfilled but asking — no — *commanding* me to come, and already I saw Rosewood hovering over the horizon, its iron-wrought gates creaking open over a dirt road flanked by bluebonnet fields.

Even over the stench of spilled Meindl coffee, I smelled wet pine wafting through the wind and felt dust catching in my throat as, silently, I shivered in anticipation of her embrace.

"I've been wanting to invite you for a while, but I wasn't sure if you would want to, and then with this pandemic, I thought you wouldn't want to leave, but," she sighed, breaking her speech with what sounded like a sip of coffee but I suspected was wine, "I miss you, and I worry about you. You'd be safer here, and it's just me here, so you'd have plenty of space."

She and her husband had divorced, but not too long afterward, he died of a concoction of carelessness and cocaine, leaving his ex-wife more widow than divorcée in the oversized house that had once been his family estate.

"You can stay as long as you like. You wouldn't have to pay rent, and you could use one of the extra rooms as a studio."

I knew there would be a *but*, and I held my breath as I waited for it.

"But I want you to paint a portrait."

Of my muse, or so my critics said, even though I'd never painted her.

Other offers and demands had been made. Agents who said it would sell were promptly fired, circulating more theories about my traumatic past.

Supposedly I'd already completed a portrait and was saving it for when the value had exponentially increased or I became broke like all artists eventually did. One critic suggested I was so deranged I slept with this fictitious portrait, failing to disclose in his review that I'd declined his demand for sex.

Emily rambled on with incentives and requests, promising to pay more than I received for any other painting and supplementing my humble salary from the art magazine I edited, but I knew there would never be enough money to paint what she wanted and that, at the same time, any money would be more than enough.

When I still did not answer, she offered me time to think, but my mind was made. My certainty startled her, so she kept providing reassurances.

"If you start and find it's too difficult, you can stop, and I'd understand. I'd still pay for your time."

The desperation in her voice would have persuaded anyone.

I reassured her that I would accept, but she insisted I wait a few days before committing.

It was an emotional day, and she didn't want that to influence my decision.

I laughed to myself, thinking she hadn't even heard about Hélène, for which I was glad she hadn't because otherwise she would insist I take more time, and I didn't want to waste another second in Vienna.

Again, I promised her I would come, and we hung up with our usual "I love you" but without our standard sorrow.

Still, I was sad.

Sad about Hélène, sadder that it had taken me so long to reach a place I didn't want to be, and perhaps saddest that the seven years of wandering and waiting were over.

Since I couldn't bring myself to drink on that day, I brewed a cup of tea so hot it nearly burned my taste buds while gazing through a dusty window over a city I'd nearly decided to call home.

From where I stood at the window, I saw the coffee house where I had first met Hélène when she was still pretending to love men. Around the corner was the museum where we'd had our first date, and across the river were the steps of the opera house where we'd first kissed before parting in the rain, her in a taxi and me by foot to this apartment, where we'd lived pretending to be in love, where I'd loved many women while pretending to live.

In all that time and in all those places, another woman had been inhabiting my skin, making love to women who would satiate her sex, eating food that would fill her stomach, creating art that would soothe yet never satisfy her soul, suppressing and stifling sorrow she knew would have destroyed me, preserving me to return to Rosewood and to Emily, to shed a skin of seven years, and to crawl back into Eleanor.

CHAPTER TWO

M uscles fought bones as, for the first time in seven years, I set eyes upon the woman I loved as my own mother, and after the adrenaline faded, my breaths steadied, and I feared embracing her.

Thousands of miles and thirty-three hours separated Vienna and Rosewood, but we were in a pandemic. The disease that had sent the world into chaos could cling to me, and when I saw the toll that age had taken on Emily, I feared my touch might consume her.

The lines around her eyes had deepened, and her skin, thinner than I remembered, sagged from the shoulders to which it had once clung, hardly hiding the lean tendons that supported a slim body with a never-altering aesthetic of a straight, blonde bob with millimeter-measured edges framing minimalistic but bold makeup that accentuated her pale but blushing face.

Emily Pontell had been twenty-five when Eleanor was born and hadn't completed menopause by the time her daughter died.

Now, at fifty-seven, her hair was grown and grayed, her skin wrinkled and weakened. She still stood tall and proud in leather cowgirl boots that widened the difference in our height from six to seven inches, maybe seven and a half if I wasn't wearing sneakers.

Behind her hovered a house that had survived over a hundred years of Pontell heartaches, a home so grand that anyone except the Pontells wouldn't dream of living in it, save in the sense that plebians fantasized about dwelling in a castle full of ghosts.

Aside from her slower pace, Emily displayed no signs of living alone in a haunted house, nor did she display concern for disease as, the second her boots struck the ground, her arms flung and captured me so tightly I was incapable of any movement save squirming until her embrace softened the tension in my muscles as I forgot the pestilence-ridden city I'd left behind and remembered how sweet it was to be held for a purpose other than lust.

"Oh, Kitty! I've missed you so much!" she cried. I nearly wept at the sensation of hearing my name properly pronounced in her familiar Southern twang.

She pulled back, I thought to release me, but instead, she gripped me firmly by the shoulders and pressed her lips into my cheek before her sparkling eyes scanned up and down to see what changes had been forced upon a body she must have remembered as younger and prettier than the one standing before her.

I can't say what external changes I'd endured.

I didn't dwell on appearances, and most of my old photos contained Eleanor, so I didn't look at them and thus had little comparison between the woman I saw when I looked in the mirror to the girl Emily remembered.

There were doubtless more lines around my eyes, though there'd always been an indentation by my right eyebrow that my mother claimed came from thinking too much, but it had never made me look old except when working, though nowadays my mind never stops working and my manner has become brusque and distant, but it also could have been the months of lockdown that made me uneasy in her presence, and not because it was her presence but merely *a* presence.

Nevertheless, Emily exclaimed that I was all grown up and squeezed my hands as though to preserve what bits of little girl lingered before grabbing one of my bags. I'd given away most of my possessions to Hélène's friends, making me feel poor as I ascended the polished steps that would have made anyone except a Pontell feel like a peasant.

As hardwood creaked underneath my step, I stopped, startled by the changes that, though subtle, were enough to slow my pace as I wandered through Rosewood's vast rooms and wondered who I had been when antlers mounted the walls, whether the dark leather furniture had disappeared when Eleanor had died or Thomas, who Emily was now that she lived among abstract art and monochromatic furniture, who I would become amidst this foreign yet familiar place.

In the living room, where a ghastly oil portrait trying to look like something from another century had once hovered behind the piano, now hung a black-and-white photograph that was easily overlooked given the majesty of the fireplace that had once been overshadowed by the painting.

"I can take it down, if you want. And the others," Emily offered.

She'd warned me my artwork was on display, primarily pieces from when I was still in school. Throughout my career, she'd been my greatest supporter. I never asked why she bought which pieces she did, and she claimed, of course, to like all my work, but I suspected she picked the ones that reminded her most of Eleanor, though only the two of us would have seen Eleanor in that image of a blurred Berlin brothel, a place Eleanor had never been and never would have gone and a place I would never have visited if she'd still been alive.

I shook my head, stating that this was Emily's home.

"I want you to feel at home," she said, reassuringly rubbing her hand along my spine before we continued through hallways adorned with artists more famous than I would ever be and abundantly absent of Eleanor.

The door to Eleanor's old room was shut, as she'd preferred, and there was still the poster we'd made in middle school. A *Room of Eleanor's Own* was written in my exaggerated attempt at calligraphy. Underneath Eleanor's even computer-like print, it read (KITTY'S CAGE). Though it had never seemed a cage until now, not because I was inside, but because I wasn't.

"You can go in, if you'd like. Not now, but later, if you think it'll help with your work. I thought about moving things out before you came, or letting you stay there, but it didn't seem right. Nothing's changed. Except the closet's been organized."

I'd never stayed in any other room, though luckily there was no shortage of space at Rosewood. When Emily showed me a bedroom bigger than my entire apartment in Vienna, I wished I'd asked to move in long ago.

She mistook my silence for disappointment, but I assured her I was pleased, only overwhelmed, I admitted as I fiddled with the curtains, gazing out the polished windows to the empty fields where, halfway between the house and the river, stood the barn.

It hadn't been painted since I'd seen it last, and depending on the lighting, it was either an eyesore or the accentuation of Western aesthetic.

Vanishing in the distance, two girls approached, dirty river water dripping from their tangled hair as their giggles were lost under the uneven clanging of cowbells, their hands intertwining and separating and coming together again as they chased one another across the field, ignoring the calls from the house that supper was ready and avoiding thorny bushes because of their bare feet, not fearing that they might be seen as they let their bodies and love flow as freely as the breeze brushing their skin.

I released the curtain from my fingers and rested my hand over my heart, reaching through my chest for their lighthearted love. Years weighed down what those girls had shared, and I found myself clenching an empty fist.

Emily stood behind me, her chin nearly resting on the crown of my head.

I don't know what she saw, but I don't doubt the landscape was just as beautiful. I suspect the two little girls might even have been the same because, as she had then, she leaned down to tug at my ear like

I was little, kissing my cheek and then saying it was time for dinner.

The meal surpassed my culinary standards, outshining the stews and schnitzels to which I'd become accustomed to with the dish's spice and surprising simplicity.

Years of living in Texas couldn't remove the Cajun in Emily Pontell, who'd been born and reared in a home equally as grand as Rosewood except in Acadian fashion, far from the reaches of cities that would have corrupted her country cooking and isolated from people who might have made her self-conscious of her Southern style, slow as though her guests had hours to sit at a table, overbearing as though they were still starving at the end of every course, selfless as though she hadn't spent hours stirring a roux and standing at the stove on sore feet, never minding that my food was never finished despite her insistence that I needed to build up my strength, offering to fix yet another dish if I didn't like this one as she opened a second bottle of wine.

We laughed loudly, spoke more freely with every glass.

The evening was quiet compared with the days we'd dined with Eleanor.

With every offer her mother made, I heard Eleanor bicker that Emily was hovering or heard a teenage Eleanor beg for permission to eat in front of the television like at my house, to which Emily responded by saying we were welcome to eat at my house under my mother's rules, which were more restrictive than hers and which she knew we wouldn't choose because my mother couldn't cook and, while she didn't hover, wouldn't have allowed half the things permitted at Rosewood and threatened spankings if we misbehaved, though my parents wouldn't have dared touch a Pontell, earning me a double whooping for both of us once Eleanor was gone.

I never asked anything of Emily, nor did I complain or protest when she adjusted my hair or kissed my cheek, which she did more that day than she ever had, making up for seven years of missing maternal touch and months without contact save for Hélène's.

We didn't speak of Emily's dead ex-husband, whom I had only seen once since Eleanor's death, shortly after the funeral when I came to say I was going abroad again and bid farewell. He'd been drunk and hardly said a word, unable to hate me despite the wicked deed I'd done them, for which I wanted to apologize since such sentiment was long overdue, yet Emily never mentioned anything from that part of our past.

Nor did we speak of the family I didn't speak to, nor of the friends I didn't have, nor the lovers I wish I hadn't.

We didn't discuss the pandemic or politics, or even art or the portrait and purpose for which I had come.

We talked about nothing at all, but by excluding the things that mattered most, we talked about everything and understood what we wanted to say about those things we couldn't bring ourselves to mention.

We would, eventually.

It was the purpose of my return, of my art, and of my wanderings. It was the reason she remained at Rosewood, and the rationale of the invitation.

Eleanor was the essence of our existence.

Mentioning her would be like bringing up that we both breathed and that without her, we were living off our last oxygen tank.

With so little air, words became precious, so we spared them, speaking through skin in a language with neither conjugations nor declinations to confuse our affection, no genders to confine the grammar of love, with syntax so strong it carried through our conversation to the comforts of cotton sheets where even though I slept with emptiness on either side, I wasn't alone and would whisper to the ghost under the sheets, "Eleanor."

CHAPTER THREE

E leanor," I whispered, moaned, and cried in sleep and sleepless nights when she came to me, calling and crawling under my skin in a state between waking and dreaming in which I knew not whether it was her touch or the hauntings of Rosewood that stroked the sides of my shoulders, kissing me softly and then passionately until her voice woke me with the breaking of dawn and I was thrust, gasping and grasping into fresh morning air as I peeled sticky, sweaty underwear from still still-warm skin and rushed to dress for my habitual run and sole escape from the shadows of nightmares that lurked under my skin the rest of the day.

Even when Hélène had slept by me, or when other lovers like Lana had shared my bed, their touch never soothed my stress as exercise could.

Without the partial release stemming from their touch, only with movement could my body become light and senseless as I ran across the ranch, looping around the river and through the woods to avoid the barn.

Cities had robbed me of my sense of space, and months in lockdown had soured my taste for confined closed streets. City parks, once oases in urban deserts, seemed but a speck of sanity, if not pure illusion, when compared with the raw nature that surrounded Rosewood like a Western jungle for further than I could endure running in any direction.

When I returned to Rosewood with a different species of sweat than that with which I'd woken, Emily would be fixing breakfast. By the time I'd showered and washed away sweats of all sorts, she would be waiting with a cup of coffee and a plate of eggs.

Emily never spoke in the morning until she finished the paper. Since she despised electronics at the table, I skimmed the arts and culture section. There was actual news I should have been reading, but I was sick of stories about sickness and even sicker of politics, though sadly, these, too, were the selected subjects for the arts section, as though artists' lives during a pandemic were more interesting than our lives otherwise or any different than the lives of everyone else, or as though to prove that even artists, customarily considered immune to ordinary struggles, could not escape the nonsense of the pandemic and upcoming election.

Yet Emily never tired of her routine or reminding me to finish my food, so we fell into a rhythm that reflected the one of my childhood, except this time there was no school and no life outside the boundaries of the ranch.

A few days after I'd settled in, we worked out the details of the portrait.

Artistic decisions were entrusted to me.

Emily's only request was a painting.

When that painting was finished or how much it cost was of little consequence.

Such freedom was every artist's dream, though it was not that, nor even the luxury that living with Emily provided, which I treasured.

Every morning when I came to the table, she lifted her cheek for a kiss, and every evening before I went to bed, she held me tight, stroked my hair, and wished me good night.

Now more than ever I prized her motherly touch. We resurrected the affection we'd shared when I'd practically lived as her second daughter, only our conversations were punctuated by pauses in which we pretended we were not living under the shadow of terrific and terrible trauma.

"Have you told your family you're here?" She asked me one morning when the paper evidently contained nothing interesting enough to capture her attention. I'd been home for about a week and was finally beginning to adjust from jet lag.

"We don't talk."

Emily folded the financial pages. "Have you told anyone you're here?"

"Who would I tell?"

"Lana?"

Until Hélène, there was only one other serious lover aside from Eleanor. Lana and I began before Eleanor died and ended when she did.

Unfortunately, the relationship had been just about as scandalous as mine and Eleanor's. Lana was an actress and had been married to a man. Both she and her husband became even more famous after a sex tape of the two of us was released, revealing Lana's sexuality alongside her infidelity.

We still kept in touch.

It was impossible not to in our close-knit artistic circles.

"I actually did mention it to her," I admitted, "but she's not even in the U.S." Like most artists, Lana lived in no fixed location and oscillated between L.A. and London.

"What about friends?" Emily suggested as she picked up the newspaper again, pretending to skim the sports section even though she hated sports.

"I don't have any of those."

"You had friends in school." Friends other than Eleanor, she meant but wouldn't say. "And there was that boy you dated."

"I don't date boys anymore."

"You don't have to date him," she laughed, taking the art section from me and folding it in as she had the others. "Besides, I think he's married."

Though Emily and I had never acknowledged the extent of my

closeness with Eleanor, she'd known, and now my sexuality was no secret to the whole world, even though I had never officially come out to anyone.

"Have you been seeing anyone?" she asked.

I was tempted to lie, to tell her that there hadn't been anyone significant since Eleanor. Until Hélène, I could honestly say there hadn't, but that was worse than confessing my heartache.

"I was living with a girl named Helen. Hélène, as she would say. She was French. Is French," I corrected myself. She belonged to my past, but she didn't belong in the past tense. "An actress. I suppose I have a thing for them. But she left me."

"I'm sorry."

"It wouldn't have worked out. She only moved in with me because of the lockdown."

Emily started sipping her second cup of coffee, curling her fingers around the mug as she leaned back into a chair too expensive to be as ordinary as it was. "Did you love her?"

"In a way, but not in the way she wanted." Nor in the way I'd wanted or that any woman wanted. A man might have loved her as I had, but no woman wanted to be loved as a man loves, the only potential attraction being the intensity of fleeting, physical passion defined by his needs and accentuated by the climax.

"Have you been seeing anyone?" I asked though I knew the answer would be no. Hearing her admit it affirmed my own lack of a relationship.

"No," she answered with a slight shake of her head, "a few affairs and one-night stands, but nothing serious, and nothing at all since the start of this." *This* so clearly referred to the pandemic that it needed not to be stated. "I slept with Thomas right before he died. He stayed here after his mother's funeral. Actually, every time we saw each other, we ended up having sex."

She showed no shame in her confession, only reflection.

She'd never been shy about sex, often sharing gritty, intimate details that fascinated and shocked me, considering my parents didn't dare utter the word intercourse.

"I never stopped loving him," she went on, "Not even when I was signing the divorce papers."

"Do you miss him?" I asked, trying to imagine what Thomas would have been like without his daughter.

He had failed as a father, distant and apathetic as though suffering from unrequited love. I was surprised that his suppressed affection let him survive as long as he had after she died.

"Yes, but I'm also glad he's not here. I mean, I'm not happy about what happened to him, and I'm not glad he's dead, but if he were still alive, I think I would be stuck. I like to think that now he's free."

Her hand reached across the table, and I took it in mine, returning the squeeze of her fingers.

"I'm very glad you came, Kitty."

I blushed as though I'd received a compliment I didn't know how to handle. Smiling, Emily leaned forward, taking my ear lobe and wiggling it before she kissed my cheek and got up to clean the dishes.

The day wouldn't be wasted on reminiscing, and Emily's couldn't be as laid-back as mine.

She spent nearly every hour of daylight working on the ranch even though she didn't need to considering the number of workers who came.

The house was no longer what it had been in the days of real ranching. It hadn't been for nearly a hundred years since oil had been struck, and I doubted much money was made from the land anymore, but even if it was, Emily wouldn't have needed it. Her labor was one of love.

"I was thinking of going into town today," I said as I stood to bring my plate to the dishwasher.

"What for?"

"To see how it's changed," I shrugged, "Besides, I need shampoo."

"I put lots of shampoo in your bathroom."

"I know, but I'm used to cheap shampoo."

"Alright. There's a few things I need. Let me give you a list and my credit card."

"I can pay for groceries," I insisted, but she gave me her card anyway. Given the state of my bank account and the quality of groceries Emily was accustomed to, I didn't object, and within the hour, I was driving down the same dirt road I'd driven up days ago, heading to a town where I felt a foreigner but where I'd once and would again call home.

Home and town were words too strong to describe the Texas crossroads that, in my memory, consisted of country necessities: a grocery store, post office, and a gun outlet.

The nearest homes were miles away, and they only belonged to the same zip code because of politics.

Neither Emily nor anyone else I knew would ever refer to themselves as residents of this town.

We lived in the country, where a town, even as small as the speck in small print on the map, could never be considered home, not when home was defined by land and family.

I wouldn't dare call Rosewood my home.

Unless I were to marry or live long enough to be an old cat lady whose decrepit house could be considered hers, it would be wrong for me to not eternally refer to my great-grandfather's house as home.

My brothers still called it home, and my sisters, though married, I assumed, felt more connection to recollections of cramped bedrooms and crowded dinner tables than when they considered their own houses even though I should have been the one to claim the place.

Of the seven children my mother had brought into the world, only I had been born under warm incandescent bulbs instead of harsh hospital lighting, having come too quickly at the most inconvenient hour, the breaking of dawn on the morning of a hunt when, in pursuit of a buck, my father left his wife with his mother who couldn't see well enough to drive, never suspecting this child wouldn't be as punctual as her predecessors.

Of my early years I can't remember anything except my grandmother. I can't say why, but even before she died, I practically fled to the Pontells, clinging to Eleanor the second she let me borrow her colored pencil set in the first grade.

Perhaps even then, I knew I would come to reject my family's religion and conservatism and that they would detest my degenerate art and even more degenerate lifestyle.

Maybe I was inherently different, inherently gay, or inherently an artist.

Or maybe Eleanor had taught me to be everything they were not. Maybe if I'd never left, I could have come to consider these crossroads a home, but after Vienna, and before that Paris and London and Rome, not even this town, with its addition of fast-food franchises and an oversized sporting goods store, could be considered civilization.

It crossed my mind that I might run into my family, but they lived half an hour from the grocery store and nearly a full hour from the Pontells. This distance had seemed ordinary to me until it stunned my cosmopolitan friends, who found this commute unfathomable despite having hour-long metro rides.

I, too, would have now found it frustrating had it not been years since I had seen so much space.

When I stepped into the store, I was, for the first time since the start of the pandemic, thankful for masks.

I didn't want to be seen, least of all recognized.

For years, my grocery shopping had been confined to urban store-fronts in which goods were squished so closely together that it wouldn't have surprised me if they exploded, so it was impossible to comprehend the surplus of what was, by Texan standards, small.

Section after section carried brands I'd never heard of or forgotten existed, enticing me with childhood recollections so sugary my tongue tingled, enchanting me with cartoon characters too thin to represent consumers of the pictured product.

Emily's list restrained me from tossing these temptations into the cart.

She maintained a strict diet, and she would criticize me if I faltered from it.

However, it didn't restrict me from turning up and down every aisle, leaving no piece of produce unexamined, no price tag unadmired.

I followed no logical order, not pursuing the standard path that began with produce and ended with dairy and frozen foods, instead flowing through the store as though dancing with its offerings until I came to my ordained aisle.

A waft wove its way across baskets and bottles, wandering through the synthetic fabric of my mask to the edge of my nose, breaching the barrier of FFP-2 protection.

I assumed one of the bottles must have broken and spilled on the floor, but the tiles were bare, the shelves pristine.

A man brushed past me, but such an aroma couldn't be masculine.

It had to be her, the woman at the other end of the aisle with long, tangled hair and a bright blue employee vest.

In my counter-aestheticism, I insisted moments like this were an illusion of chemicals conjured from fond recollections and unfulfilled fantasies.

Her hair was nothing like mine. It was dark, unruly, and damaged from dyeing. Nevertheless, I listened when she, sensing my confusion, suggested the product she used. As though she possessed the authority of a preacher, I threw the bottles into my basket. I began to ask her some stupid questions about hair, but the intercom interrupted me, and she offered an apology, saying she better go help at customer service.

I'm a customer! I wanted to scream but couldn't.

The remainder of my shopping experience was checking things off

Emily's list as fast as I could so I could reach customer service with another insane question that would make me sound like an idiot but would give me a reason to smell her again.

But by the time I'd filled my basket with organic vegetables, given up on finding fair-trade coffee, and reached the check-out, the woman I wanted was disappearing through automatic doors.

My heart followed her, but my body wasn't brave enough to chase her through the parking lot and abandon my groceries.

At the counter, the woman raised her eyebrow as the receipt printed. "You ain't Emily Pontell."

"No," I explained, "I'm staying with her."

I would have offered more information, but the worker asked for my name and I.D. I gave my name and, as it was spoken, handed the I.D. to trembling hands leading up to eyes that refused to meet mine.

As I walked away, whispers echoed over the dinging of items passing over the scanner.

My name had been remembered.

I stepped outside and pulled my mask from my face, scanning the parking lot for a head of dark, messy hair. Nearly every spot was empty, and the only person was the one entering the store.

"Kitty?"

I narrowed my eyes, trying to imagine how this woman would have looked fifteen years ago. She said something about school without offering her name. As the lines in her face faded, I saw a cheerleader with what would have then been naturally blonde hair and an equally false voice. She asked if I was visiting family, and I stumbled over an answer that mentioned Rosewood and work without giving names or details. She nodded and flashed a bleached, strained smile.

"I've heard about your art. You've made quite a name for yourself."

As though I hadn't had a name before.

"Would you like to come out for dinner with us this weekend? I bet you miss a good ol' Texas steak."

"Us?" I asked, imagining suffering at a table with soccer moms overtipping for cheap cocktails.

"Oh, I thought you would have heard," she laughed, "Chrisopher and I got married. We have two kids."

"Congratulations," I answered automatically, unable to muster either enthusiasm or annoyance about my first and only boyfriend's marital status.

"If it'd be weird for you, I understand."

"No, I don't care." I shook my head. "But, sure, yeah, that'll be nice."

It wouldn't, so I don't know why I said I would or why, when she called the next day, I didn't pretend to have plans for the weekend. I didn't want to see her or anyone else from the past, not when they weren't crucial for the portrait.

They weren't part of Eleanor's past, which meant they couldn't be part of mine unless I was wrong about the history of my life and that there was more to my past than hers, more to my purpose here than a portrait, but in the end, it was merely an excuse, but I wasn't sure what for, and Emily gave me a disapproving look when I told her I was meeting them for dinner.

"This morning you said you didn't have any friends."

"She and I weren't really friends."

"And I thought you didn't care about Christopher."

"I never had sex with him," I stated as though this supported my decision.

"I know."

Heat rushed to my cheeks. Of course she did. She was the only one who'd heard about my first time with a man. Eleanor had argued about it with me in front of Emily, though I hadn't even told Eleanor and never learned how she found out.

Christopher was a chauvinist, and his hyper-masculinity had attracted me as an alternative to Eleanor's femininity, a test of sexuality set up to fail. I was surprised even a straight woman could stand him. Now,

I would have to suffer him for an evening alongside a woman with the only flavor of femininity that could cater to his fetishes: prissy ponytails and pink lipstick.

"Will it bother you if I go?" I asked.

"Why would it bother me?"

"Because," I paused, searching for a reason, "there's a pandemic?"

"And do I seem very concerned about it?"

"No, but-"

"But you want an excuse not to go, so if you want me to pretend it bothers me, I can."

"It doesn't bother me because of the pandemic."

Emily smiled, looking at me with one of those maternal looks that reveals and asks everything while saying nothing, permitting me to pour out my problems or to preserve silence, whichever I preferred. With my own mother, I inevitably chose silence. Still, with Emily, I couldn't speak enough, except I didn't tell her about the woman in the shampoo aisle, which, at the time, I thought I would soon forget.

"They weren't nice to her when we were in school. Or about us," I admitted.

"Then they weren't nice to you either."

"No, I suppose not."

"Then why do you want to go?"

"To see if they've changed? To see if I've changed."

"You're a world-class artist. They're still stuck in the middle of Texas."

"You and I are in the middle of Texas," I countered, realizing that no matter how much I wanted to pretend I'd gotten away, my heart was stuck. If I didn't face them, it always would be.

Chapter Four

E scape had come through art since before I could remember. From fantastical finger paintings to psycho-sexual photographs, realms forged in creativity provided refuge from the harsh reality of my family's farm and its self-imposed suppression.

Very few of my works remained from the five years of my life before I met Eleanor, and I wasn't desperate enough to journey home and search through my family's mess to find them. I doubted I would be able to distinguish them from another toddler's scribblings, at least not until the drawings from the day after Eleanor had lent me her colored pencils.

She appeared in each of my pictures after that.

We couldn't have been more than stick figures then or even months and years later when I discovered depth and perception and used her as my model for mastering techniques.

After my grandmother gave me my first camera, Eleanor and I became Polaroids, and after Emily gave me my first SLR, Eleanor became a darkroom beauty, a muse captured with the click of a shutter and held between chemical-softened fingers, the ideal feminine to whom I made love under film sheets and caressed with heavy brush strokes.

Now, my creations were as devoid of life as the house Caroline and Christopher pretended to live in by calling it their home, each of them as desperate for love as the children they pretended not to loathe.

At the last minute, they switched the location of our planned dinner from a restaurant to their house, claiming their babysitter had Covid. I suspected they either didn't want to be seen with me or that they wanted to show off their decadent house.

"I heard you're a lesbian," their daughter said not even two minutes into our meal.

Christopher slugged back beer as Caroline discreetly informed the girl that she was being rude.

"My grandma says lesbians are going to hell," the boy continued, and his mother insisted he hush and looked desperately to her husband and then apologetically to me as they sipped generously from their expensive alcohol.

"Why does she say that?" I asked as I sliced my meat, looking so directly in the children's eyes they squirmed and looked to their parents for help. No one answered, so I asked, "Do you know what a lesbian is?"

Christopher coughed, glancing away as he murmured in a half-comprehensible tone that conveyed his attitude louder than his words. "They're a bit young for that."

His wife attempted to compensate with a pre-prepared explanation. "Just like Mommy and Daddy love each other, Kitty loves women."

The comparison made me want to vomit, but I grinned through clenched teeth as though to thank her.

"Does that mean you kiss girls?" the daughter asked, her gaze shifting from her mother to me.

I said yes, and she gave a slight nod, expressing she had unlocked another little piece of adult wisdom.

"Kissing boys sounds gross. I think I'll be a lesbian, too."

Christopher broke into further coughing. Caroline's face flushed as she rushed to say, "You're too young for kissing, honey. You don't need to decide yet."

The boy spoke over her. "If I kiss girls, would I be a lesbian?"

"No, sweetheart, that's normal."

As the insult was recognized, Caroline turned to me and began apologizing. I shook my head and excused her concerns, claiming it didn't bother me, comforting her by changing the subject to something dull.

The conversation was a dance, a Texas two-step around issues we knew would insult our partners, a Southern waltz with fancy footing that forgave a few missteps so long as they were quickly and quietly corrected.

We joked about politics without specifying which candidates we found repulsive by calling both parties corrupt, invoked religion with the piety of memorized quotes, generalizing our opinions so they met instead of collided in the middle of the road.

In Europe, I complained about conversations characterized by colonial conventionalism. Still, after years of continental confrontation, I craved shallow comforts coupled with crispy chicken and cavity-creating tea and overlooked Caroline and Christopher's conservatism.

I had no desire to be a crusader for my sexuality.

Not even when I'd been in the comforts of Europe or the safety of creative society did I broach the subject. On occasion, I complained about straight men or offered an opinion on the latest queer story in the news, but asking about my experience was the best way to close me up as tight as a clam.

I wished, that night, to let myself go so far as to forget about art and Eleanor and escape into the comforts of company and children.

I was so out of practice communicating with kids that I didn't dumb things down the way adults usually did, making me so popular I was granted a good night kiss from each kid when Christopher was gentlemanly enough to help them get ready for their bedtime, giving us girls time to chat, offering with a grin that made it seem as though tucking his own offspring into bed was a gallantly selfless act.

Just one glance at the couple made it clear they were stuck in another century's gender roles.

Throughout dinner, I'd warmed up to Caroline out of pity and nostalgia, so I was glad for the moment without male company.

She offered me wine, but I declined since I had to drive. She offered the guest room, but I hadn't warmed up to her that much.

And as soon as she offered, I'd itched for the soft sheets at Rosewood and decided to hurry up with my dessert without being rude.

"I'm sorry about earlier," she apologized. "Christopher's mother heard you were coming and threw a fit about homosexuality and hell. She's from another generation, you know."

It was true, but it was also her generation that had lived through the seventies.

I held my tongue and complimented Caroline's children, saying they were lucky to have such great parents even though I knew that in thirty years, the kids would be just as corrupted by convention as their parents and that hoping for anything original from either child was unrealistic. Though to be fair, my upbringing had not been so different, only with louder prayers and with less money.

"The twins were an accident," she admitted when Christopher was out of earshot. "That's why we got married. He didn't want to." She leaned in, glancing to the stairs to see if he would come down. "He didn't want them. He was seeing another girl and was planning on leaving me."

The drinks were beginning to work. She poured herself another glass.

I began to worry she'd mistaken my warmth for authentic friendship, but her misery was entertaining, so I played along.

"Really?" I asked with a false gasp. There was no surprise in what she said. They fated themselves to infidelity back when we were in high school and he threw a football and she tossed a pompom, sealing their fate further when he tore his ACL in college and she joined a sorority.

I imagined Eleanor pretending to gag as Caroline continued, making faces at her when she wasn't looking so only I could see while she playing footsie with me under the table.

"Next thing you know he'll be screwing his secretary," she said as she rolled her eyes in a way that suggested he probably already was. "You know it really shook him up to learn you were a lesbian. He kept worrying he'd done something wrong to crew you up. Not that being gay is screwed up! But, he was worried he hadn't performed well and that it had changed your mind."

He hadn't performed well, nor had we ever had actual sex, but I let her ramble on the shortcomings of men with her proud, insightful tone that made it seem as though she had discovered the secrets other women had known for all of history.

He would never please her, but he could maybe curtail insanity by offering an orgasm now and again.

"Can you read them a bedtime story?" Christopher asked, his heavy feet creaking hardwood hidden underneath carpet as he descended a staircase trying to mimic Rosewood's.

All the big homes in the area tried to copy Rosewood.

Caroline sighed and apologized to me before muttering something to her husband on her way up. He shook his head with less grace than her eye roll and poured himself a more potent drink than hers before sitting across from me.

"Have fun complaining about me?" he teased, flashing a grin while leaning back in his chair and fanning out his arms to hold his head between his hands to display how much space he could and would take up.

"What would I have to complain about?"

He laughed as he sipped his whiskey. "You know, I guessed there was something off about you when we were together."

"Off?"

"Well, different. I could tell you weren't into me. You being a lesbian makes sense."

"Because otherwise I would have been interested in you?"

"Well, yeah. Of course."

"Of course?"

"What do you mean?"

"Just because a woman isn't a lesbian doesn't mean she's automatically attracted to you."

"I know that," he said with a scoff that suggested he didn't believe it.

He drank more whiskey as the alcohol he'd already downed kicked in harder. He made more insensitive jokes and references to how he was much more accepting than his parents and grandparents about that sort of thing, praising himself on his progress and recognition of white male privilege, which must have sounded honest as it echoed into his own ears.

He even had the audacity to lean in close, looking over his shoulder to ensure his wife wasn't there when he whispered, "You know, if you ever wanted to give it a shot, I wouldn't mind. Caroline might even be into it. She liked that video of you. Lana Lane. Sexy."

"It's getting late. I should head home."

He chuckled, shaking his head as though my rejection were like turning down an offer to sleep with a god. "I knew you were still hung up on that crazy bitch."

Before I could think up a coherent answer, whiskey was splashed in his face. As he screamed how expensive it had been, all I could think was that I wished it had cost more and that I should have broken something or shouted a witty insult, but that he wasn't worth a second more of my time.

If I'd been as brave as Eleanor would have wanted me to be, I would have spat the truth in his face and told him the only reason I dated him was that my father hit me when he found Eleanor and me kissing. I thought going out with him would be better than a black eye, but I was wrong, and at least with a black eye, I would have had trouble seeing his face.

Instead, I left without a word.

His wife's yelling stopped him from coming after me, but it didn't do anything to stop me from marching to my car without turning back to face her apology. She was crying, desperate for me to stay so we could talk so she could feel better about herself.

"Your husband just asked me to have sex with him," I told her as I climbed into my car.

"What? No, you must have misunderstood."

I shut the door, refusing to roll down my window and acknowledge her excuses that he was drunk. Instead, I offered a look that said I was sorry, not for what I'd done, but for how pathetic her life had become and that I had to drive back through the terrible town she called home, too numb to cry as I changed the radio station until I found something other than country, swearing as I saw the tank was nearly empty and pulled into the only place that sold gasoline at midnight.

A young couple was making out on the other side of the pump.

I pictured Eleanor's hands sliding over mine as she leaned close to whisper that seeing me so aggressive had turned her on that she couldn't wait until we made it home.

I pushed open my door. The couple pulled apart. The boy muttered something about grabbing cigarettes, and I tuned them out as I picked up the pump and opened the gas cap. Once he was gone, I caught the whiff I couldn't forget, and I poked my head around the no-smoking sign.

She pulled the nozzle from the car and returned it to the handle, her eyes flickering up and catching mine. Her hand hesitated on the handle. It was the young woman from the grocery store with coconut-scented hair.

Her eyes were puffy, her skirt out of sorts.

"You're Kitty Kunz," she said, her voice half a gasp.

"How do you know that?"

Her cheeks brightened, and her gaze dropped as she tucked a tangled strand of hair behind her ear. She was younger than I'd thought in the shampoo aisle, but she'd been wearing a mask then. Now I saw she was no older than twenty.

"I want to be an artist."

"Want to?"

"When I grow up," she explained, making me guess she wasn't even twenty.

"You don't become an artist. You're either are or aren't one."

"I am an artist," she insisted with enough force that I believed her.

The pump clicked, and I yanked it from the car to return it to the pump. The door to the store dinged. Reaching into my wallet, I removed a card and held it out to her.

"Give me a call and prove it. And do yourself a favor and don't smoke."

She was too shocked to thank me and then too distracted when the boy approached to look at me. I was gone before she could say anything else, but with my window rolled down, I could hear her decline the cigarette. When I turned out of the parking lot, my mind was already spinning in anticipation of the painting that would keep me up until dawn.

CHAPTER FIVE

I f ever Eleanor had opened her front door and been as captivated by my face as I was with the grin that greeted me as I welcomed my guest to Rosewood, I could die content even if my art never captured the rapture I sought to express and which I never thought I would feel from Eleanor's side of the front door.

The girl seemed even younger than she'd appeared in the dark, her makeup-less sexy but infinitely more attractive, her lipstick pink instead of red, her dress classic as opposed to an attempt at chic. Her hair was every bit as tangly, still wafting with spice and waving with coconut.

"So, this is Rosewood," she said as she craned back her neck, sending shivers across my skin as I searched for an acceptable answer. "Should I take off my shoes?"

I looked down. Her sneakers looked like they'd been soaked in mud and dried out in dirt.

"Well, the floors were just cleaned."

She slid off her shoes, her cheeks flushing as she attempted to conceal her mismatched socks.

I asked if she wanted anything to drink, but she shook her head and removed the portfolio from her backpack.

She'd called the day after we'd seen each other at the gas station. We hadn't chatted long, and all I'd learned was her name.

Elisabeth Evergreen. Except she went by Sissy.

I'd invited her over without asking anything else.

"Should we go up to my studio?" I asked, and she nodded.

"I didn't realize you lived here. I mean, I knew you were from here and had heard about ... " We turned a corner, and she commented on the size of the home to save her from addressing Eleanor and saying instead, "But I thought you lived abroad."

"I do," I explained, "or at least I did until a few weeks ago. Mrs. Pontell commissioned a painting, so I moved back."

"Just for her?"

"Just for her. And for the painting."

"Where is she?"

"Out working. She does most of the work around here herself. She's a real cowgirl."

"Is that–" Sissy stopped in front of a collector's piece.

"Yes," I said, turning back from the top of the stairs. The painting wasn't famous and was one of the artist's early works. Still, it was impossible not to recognize the craftsmanship that should have been in a museum and not wasting away across from my art. "And the one opposite is mine, but no one notices."

"Oh, I'm sorry!" she exclaimed, spinning around and furrowing her eyebrows when she saw the tiny finger painting.

I didn't explain, urging her to keep up with a remark Eleanor would have made, albeit in a more annoyed tone. "Come on, it's not the Louvre."

Eleanor's ghost followed me through the halls, glaring every step of the way.

This wasn't my home. It was hers, always *hers* and never mine, even as she spoke through my lips, reciting a history that wasn't mine to claim, how the Pontells had been here since before the Texan Republic, though back then they'd had a different name.

A daughter had inherited, so the family took her husband's name while the house kept its own.

"Is that the barn where her daughter killed herself?"

We were at the door to my studio, and in the wall was a window with a perfect view of the dilapidating barn. I stopped, my hand hovering over the cold metal handle.

"There is one rule in this house. Never mention that. Especially not if Mrs. Pontell is here."

"I'm sorry."

"No," I shook my head, startled by the force of my own voice. I opened the door. "Don't be. I don't mean to be rude. It's just best to be clear from the beginning. Some people try to understand what happened, but there's nothing to understand. She was deranged and committed suicide. She just did it more dramatically than most people."

"I'm sorry."

"I just told you not to be. You didn't know her."

"No, I'm sorry for your loss."

"Oh," I shut the door behind her, keeping my head averted from the gaze I wished would shift from me to my art.

I couldn't remember the last time anyone had told me that.

Before the funeral, probably.

Afterward no one felt sorry for me, only sorry they'd been forced to listen to my inappropriate outburst after the sermon.

"It was a long time ago," I said, though it didn't seem like it.

I asked if she'd like to see what I was working on, though I added that the portrait was off-limits. At that stage it was only a series of sketches anyway.

"What are you working on? Something for your magazine?"

My primary way of paying the bills was by editing a quarterly art publication. It was new and award-winning but less prestigious now that I was the editor rather than the founder who had a permanent installation at a fancy museum and a new position at a better magazine. Still, it had steady subscribers and a stout contributor list.

"I don't put my own work in the magazine. Except the letter from the editor, and even that's heavily edited. I can show you some new photos."

"I'd love to see them," she said in a single gasp that reminded me of the first time I'd met one of my idols, a man I now knew to be a drunk who would probably be canceled if any of my straight female friends came forward with how he'd treated them.

I gestured for her to pull up a chair by the computer, relishing the tropical scent as her hair brushed past, rushing to open the files when she sat beside me lest she notice how powerfully she had overtaken my imagination.

"How old are you?" I asked while we waited for the computer to power on.

"Nineteen."

"Liar," I accused, glancing at her from the corners of my eyes. "Sixteen?"

"Seventeen," she corrected, "but I'll be eighteen next month."

"Any big plans?"

She shook her head.

"Not doing anything with your boyfriend?"

"He's not my boyfriend."

"Oh."

"He was, but he's starting college this semester, so we're keeping it casual. Grown up."

"Relationships don't get easier when you're grown up, or any more casual."

"What about you? Do you have a ..." she hesitated, and I laughed.

In Vienna, kids half her age wouldn't have hesitated to use the word girlfriend. For a second, I longed for a coffee house where I could curl up with a newspaper until Hélène finished rehearsal and met me with a kiss that no one except us cared about in a café cramped with cakes and coffee cups clinking constantly over the chatter of countless other couples.

I pictured Hélène in France, sunbathing in the countryside with her mother and complaining about me.

Outside, Eleanor's ghost looked up at me all the way from the barn, so far away I could barely see that her eyes were fixed on mine.

I clicked on a file and pushed the mouse towards Sissy, standing to close the curtains but stopping when I saw a very real Emily arguing with one of the workers and was glad I didn't have to suffer her temper and could enjoy the entertainment while waiting for Sissy to go through the photos, my heart pounding as I anticipated her reaction.

There was nothing provocative, but each photo contained a piece of me, and no matter how insignificant, my skin crawled when I thought of someone aside from Eleanor or Emily peering inside even though I knew thousands of people encountered my art in museums and that, thanks to smartphones, even more eyes stumbled across slices of my soul on screens.

"They're beautiful," I heard Sissy say, her voice trembling.

I closed the curtain, turning away from Emily and the imagined Eleanor before returning to my seat.

During the lockdowns, I had taken my fair share of typical pandemic photographs: monuments without tourists blocking the view, empty streets, masks on mannequins. They were popular, but I was glad they weren't what captivated Sissy's attention so ardently that she hovered at the edge of her seat as though trying to bring herself as close to the picture as possible without distorting its proportions.

"I don't know what to say," she admitted, unable to pull her eyes from the image.

Flattered, I reached over to take the mouse, exiting out of the image. Her eyes darted to me, and in her desperation, I saw my young, eager self, and I fed her what she wanted.

"Show me yours."

She fumbled through her backpack to find her portfolio, presenting a memory card while hurrying to explain that she didn't have a printer. I waved her worries aside, plugging the card into the computer and scanning her written work while it loaded.

"Short stories?" I asked.

"Two short stories, some poetry, and the opening to a play."

My eyes shifted as I came across the play. "Iambic pentameter?"

"Too much?" she asked nervously.

"Mhm," I muttered as I opened the file with the photos, narrowing my eyes as soon as I saw them. "Are you using a point-and-shoot?"

"That's all I have."

"Never be ashamed of your equipment, but never blame your camera for bad photos," I told her as I scrolled through, trying to keep my face as neutral as possible to hide potential displeasure.

"You have a unique eye," I complimented before asking her about her goals as an artist and the colleges she was applying to, and she was surprised when I told her not to study art. "Art professors are just failed artists. It's why they teach art," I explained, rummaging through some books and tossing her tomes of images while encouraging her to study philosophy or something useful. I stopped myself when I realized her backpack would weigh her down and that I hadn't seen a car in the driveway.

She asked when she should bring the books back, and I suggested next week but that she could keep the books as long as she wanted.

Her face brightened, but before she could thank me, there was a knock at the door.

"Come in!" I called, powering off the computer and handing Sissy her SD card, my face flushing as Emily opened the door, greeting us with the suggestive grin that had disgusted Eleanor when we were teenagers.

"Sorry. I don't want to bother, but I was wondering if your guest wants to stay for dinner."

Sissy was already standing, her eyes wider than when she'd first seen me.

"Sissy, this is Mrs. Pontell. Emily, this is -"

"Just call me Emily," Emily interrupted. Before I could get in another word, they were shaking hands and offering polite compliments about

Emily's home and Sissy's dress. When they reached the subject of supper, Sissy insisted she should get home since they always ate at seven.

"Your mom must be grateful for your help. Or your father. Whoever cooks. Kitty never helps me cook," Emily teased as we guided her to the front door.

"You never let me," I protested, "Besides, you wouldn't want me to help. I'm a terrible cook.

Sissy intervened, "I'm not that great, but it's just my dad and me at home, and he doesn't really cook, but we both like to eat."

Emily glanced over her shoulder, flashing a bright smile. "Well, you're welcome anytime." She opened the door and, after glancing around, looked strangely at Sissy. "Did you walk here?"

"No, I rode my bike," Sissy nodded to a rusting bicycle leaning against the steps.

Emily looked at Sissy's dress and laughed. "It's so hot, and you must live at least three miles from here. The bike will fit in the truck. I can drive you."

"Oh, thank you, but that's fine. I like the exercise."

I intervened. "I can drive you. Those books are heavy."

But Sissy refused, and Emily and I relented, watching with a mixture of frustration and admiration as the bicycle's thin tires bumped up and down over the gravel.

"I know I've heard the name Evergreen before," Emily murmured as she shut the door, "I'll have to ask someone. So, what's the story between you two?"

"There is no story. She's an artist. I'm an artist."

Emily laughed, rolling her eyes. "She has the same look you did when you were that age."

"What's that supposed to mean?"

"You tell me. You've got a similar look now."

"No, I don't," I protested, but then, in the same way I had when I was seventeen, I stormed off to my room and escaped into art.

Chapter Six

S issy swirled in and out and around my consciousness, swimming through somnambulist senses and surfacing in superficial sketches, stealing chalk and coveting sheets intended for the one to whom I had never sworn but held eternal devotion, who demanded I abandon the pursuit of other subjects and altered the aim of the lines I drew so that the visage I drew was never Sissy's, but Eleanor's.

I resolved after each visit that the next would be Sissy's last, but every time she came, I invited her back.

We discussed pure, innocent pieces of art, never straying into the provocative or perverse, but beneath our appropriate conversation dwelled desperation and frustration for and of something we dared not describe but sensed.

Weeks went by with a pattern in which she came almost every day, and each time, we hid away in my studio, showing each other pictures until she had to go home or to work.

Emily always came to say goodbye, giving me suggestive looks once the door was shut.

One evening, as the sun began to set, I offered to drive her home. She declined, saying she better go but lingering by asking a question I knew was but a delay, and before long, it was impossible to ignore the scents steaming from the kitchen.

When Emily knocked, she said she'd cooked for three, persuading Sissy to stay.

We went downstairs, but Sissy slipped away to call her father and let him know she'd be late.

"I asked about her family," Emily said once Sissy was out of earshot. "Her mother left when she was a baby. The father's white trash. It's amazing she's as normal as she is. I never would have known, except that her clothes are old and too small."

I'd hardly noticed her clothes, but when she came down, I was surprised I hadn't recognized that her dress was designed for a pre-pubescent girl.

If she'd been there, Eleanor would have judged her, whispered in my ear behind her back to make me laugh insecurely because I felt sorry and not silly, and because I suspected that had Eleanor's first impression of me been in my usual clothes and not a school uniform, she never would have loved me.

Emily greeted Sissy as an equal, pouring her a glass of wine and grinning as the girl giggled. After clinking glasses, Emily returned her attention to the stove, asking if she was starstruck about meeting a famous artist.

I rolled my eyes. "I'm not famous."

"You've got a Wikipedia page!" Emily insisted.

"With about three paragraphs."

"That's three more than the rest of us!"

Sissy laughed, adding, "And there's the video."

My grip on my wine glass tightened as I swallowed more.

Sissy hadn't asked about the infamous sex tape yet, but I knew it was only a matter of time.

Emily changed subjects as she saw my eyes narrow. "But, Sissy, Kitty tells me you're more into writing."

"Yes, ma'am."

"Oh, please don't call me that. It makes me feel so old," Emily said, laughing in a way that made her years seemed to vanish, the lighthearted lift in her voice taking me back to summer nights long ago, when the three of us had sat on the back porch drinking wine long past dark.

"Sorry," Sissy blushed.

"No need to apologize. It is nice to know some people still have manners. What do you like to write about?"

"Everything that's in my head. Well, not everything. That would be a bit boring."

"Not to a psychologist," Emily countered.

"It wouldn't be very exciting for psychologists since they already know what's going through people's heads.

"But I've always had the impression that artists have something different going through their heads than normal people. Otherwise they wouldn't be so extraordinary."

"Are you a musician?" Sissy asked. "I saw a piano in the other room."

"I used to play, but not anymore."

"She also plays guitar," I added.

"I haven't picked up an instrument in years," Emily shook her head and went on, "If I were to do something artistic, writing seems most natural, but I suppose that's because it's something I can already do. At least I know how to put words together and form sentences. I wouldn't know what to do with a brush except splatter paint on a canvas."

"That's what some of the most famous artists have done."

"Including Kitty when she was younger." Emily teased, "Did she tell you the story behind the finger painting in the hallway?"

I swallowed more wine as Sissy shook her head, and Emily went on.

"We went to a contemporary art exhibit, and Kitty claimed she could make art just as good, so the next time we went to the museum, she took that painting up to the curator and asked him to hang it up with the others. I thought it was so silly I decided to hang it on the wall. No one believes me when I say I like it better than the expensive paintings."

"I wish everyone thought so highly of my work," I murmured.

"Lots of people do! You had a piece in the Met!"

"One photograph from a contest. Honorable mention."

"You're always selling yourself short. Sissy, darling, you do eat meat, don't you?"

The girl nodded, and Emily winked at me. "I like her."

Sissy laughed, her eyes flickering away. "Do you have something against vegetarians?"

"I don't have anything against them, but I believe the body needs meat, and you're a growing girl. You need all the protein you can get."

"I think I'm done growing. I've been this tall for three years."

"Well, your mind needs protein to make genius art."

"I don't know about genius."

"Of course it'll be genius. I can tell you're smart. Is there anything in particular you're working on at the moment?"

"A few short stories. You can read them once they're done."

"I'd like that. Kitty, would you take these plates to the table?"

We moved to the patio, and Emily and I started eating almost as soon as we picked up our forks. Sissy hesitated, I guessed because she was accustomed to praying. I briefly considered offering to say one, but as soon as she caught me looking at her, she lowered her fork to her food, which was for the best as I wouldn't want to offend her god with false prayers.

The cicadas had begun buzzing, and in the distance, horses neighed. Sheep whined, prompting Sissy to ask about the property and animals, her eyes widening at the numbers and details about the ranch's size, reminding me that, for everyone else, stepping foot in Rosewood was like walking onto a movie set.

"Don't you get lonely out here all by yourself?" Sissy asked Emily about halfway through the meal, and I was tempted to give her a look that might remind her that the question was too personal, but Emily answered without skipping a beat.

"Sometimes, but now that Kitty's here, it's a bit like old times. Minus the crazy parties."

And Eleanor.

Emily finished her glass of wine and began to pour herself another as she continued, "If you'd like, I can show you around sometime. Do you know how to ride?"

"It's been a while," Sissy confessed.

"Well, that's not a problem. We'll take it easy. Unless you prefer the dirt bike."

Sissy laughed, shaking her head.

"Good, because I hate the noise. Bad for the environment, too."

"Then why do you have one?"

"It was my husband's. Sometimes it's handy if you need to get to the other side of the ranch quickly, but I don't enjoy riding it for fun. I'll get some more wine," she said, standing after serving us both another glass.

When she was gone, I tried to read Sissy's face.

She didn't wear her emotions bare, but youth made her vulnerable.

"We can go on a photography shoot together sometime," I offered, having rejected my resolution that this meeting would be our last the moment Sissy had entered.

"I'd like that," Sissy nodded as Emily returned with another bottle.

Emily made a few comments about the wine, but as she realized Sissy's understanding of wine was limited to red and white and that I wasn't in the mood for information I'd only half-understand, she poured it without commentary. As the evening went on, we relaxed into conversations about every possible topic except for the pandemic, giving me a glimpse of hope for what the future might hold.

Emily tired before the two of us, reminding me she wasn't as young as she had been when we'd sat out with Eleanor and drank nearly until dawn.

She asked Sissy if she preferred to stay, offering to call a taxi if she didn't. Surprisingly, Sissy accepted, and Emily asked if I could show her one of the rooms with a suggestive glimmer in her eye before kissing me goodnight and wishing Sissy sweet dreams.

Were Sissy not so young, I would have invited her to stay in my room. However, I couldn't forget that she was still a month on the wrong side of eighteen.

I couldn't tell if she was aware of my flirtations or if she was just young and overly polite; her responses were kind as opposed to infatuation.

The longer we talked, the less she held back. She still hid details, but I did the same, so we primarily discussed art. She told me the artists she admired, and they were the same ones that had fascinated me at her age—the classics, of course, which still amazed me, albeit without the thrill of novelty.

As the temperature dropped, we went inside, where I pulled out a few books to show her modern works, letting her peruse while I cleaned up.

Whenever her eyes widened or her fingers traced the glossy page as she transfixed herself on a single, subtle detail, my heartbeat quickened. I had to stabilize myself with a heavy breath.

I could have stayed awake with her for hours obsessing over art, yet after animating, wine wearies, and Sissy began to yawn. Knowing she was too polite to end our conversation, I stopped it before tiring her too much and showed her to one of the extra rooms, indicating where the bathroom and towels were, reminding her that if she needed anything, my bedroom was down the hall, and then, at the cusp of night and dawn and the threshold of a door creaked either half-open or closed, I kissed her cheek so softly and sweetly I might as well have been touching her lips.

As I felt the blood rush under my flesh, I drew my neck back, my breath catching as I began to apologize. A kiss on the cheek was common enough to excuse me, but what happened next wasn't, except it didn't come from me.

She threw her lips against mine, passionately, but withdrew before I comprehended what was happening, and she whispered goodnight in a shy, satisfied voice.

CHAPTER SEVEN

F idelity was the core of my parents' marriage. They'd met and
married in college, probably virgins since they followed the other
commandments so legalistically. Love might have been their founda-
tion once, but after children, monogamy became their pillar. No one
else could ever love them, and it was better to be possessed than lonely.

The Pontells loved each other so strongly they couldn't possess each
other, so constant in infidelity that it belonged to them as much as
faithfulness did my parents.

They never hid their affairs, nor did Eleanor hide her disdain for them,
just as she didn't hide her disgust when I was young and needed to
experiment or when she knew it was only a cover like with Christopher.

We never swore oaths or defined terms, but I always crawled back
to her and offered my body and soul on Eleanor's altar.

Only when I kissed Sissy, and I kissed her again and again after that
evening, I didn't see Eleanor.

When I went to bed, their faces alternated in my pre-dream fantasies.
I reminded myself I couldn't help myself in such a tired state, so it
couldn't count as infidelity, which was what had damaged my relationship with Eleanor more than once.

My kisses with Sissy ordinarily never went further than they had that
first time until one afternoon when we got carried away on the couch
like we were both teenagers. Our clothes were still on, but if Emily had
walked in any later, they wouldn't have been.

I jerked my body off of Sissy's, sitting up and wiping my lips as I caught my breath.

Sissy, her face flushed, jumped up. "I was just leaving!"

Opening the fridge, Emily shrugged and pulled out a pitcher of iced tea. "Don't mind me. I have work to do. I do expect that couch to be kept clean, though."

"I should get home to make dinner," Sissy insisted.

"You can invite your father over sometime if you'd like."

"I'd rather not," Sissy admitted. Her eyes drooped, and I took her hand, but she pulled it away and stuffed it in her pocket.

"Fair enough," Emily answered as she poured a glass, "but your birthday is next week. Do you want to invite some friends over?"

"No, I don't really have friends."

"That's fine. Kitty doesn't have friends either."

"Neither do you!" I protested.

Gulping her tea, Emily set the glass on the counter with a clink. "I'm middle-aged and have a huge house. I don't need friends. Anyway, Sissy, you're only turning eighteen once. What do you want to do?"

Her visits had become regular, and nearly every time, she slept over, kissing me goodnight as she had before but longer and less shyly.

When I woke, later than either her or Emily, I found the two of them chatting, Emily's face as bright as it had been since my arrival and Sissy soaking up more affection than she'd ever been granted.

Once Sissy had visited just to go riding with Emily, and they'd been gone for hours before returning home laughing harder than I thought Emily capable of, given her tragic history.

Emily learned more about Sissy than I did. I could list Sissy's favorite poets and describe her style of photography, but if you asked me her favorite food, I wouldn't have had an answer.

"You don't need to do anything for me," Sissy objected.

"Of course I do!"

"Just dinner is fine."

"Alright, but it'll be a special dinner. Think about what you want and let me know."

Sissy relented but insisted she best be going. We walked her to the door, offering again to drive her home only to be refused. Emily kissed her cheek. When Sissy hugged me, she leaned in for a kiss I wasn't expecting, and my neck yanked back. Her face flushed, and she lurked away apologetically.

My heart rushed, and in an instant, it felt as though my love depended on this kiss alone, so I seized her hand, taking her by the arm to pull her so close our chests squished, my lips pressing instead of interlocking hers.

Our eyes were open, and I saw her panic and shoved myself away, bidding goodbye as she rushed out the door.

The door slammed shut.

"I wish I could blame the pandemic for that," I murmured, thinking it might have been the worst kiss I'd ever given anyone.

"So do I," Emily sighed, her tone echoing Eleanor's schadenfreude as she pointed out, "You have lipstick on your cheek."

"Oh, sorry," I lifted my hand to wipe it off, but she stopped me.

"You'll smear it. Come here, I'll fix your hair, too."

"What's wrong with my hair?" I asked as we wandered to her bedroom.

This was the first time I'd been inside Emily's room was when returning to Rosewood. In our childhood, Eleanor and I had played dress-up in her mother's closet almost daily.

The layout remained the same, and the walls were still white, but the bed was no longer of imposing mahogany, and the Western paintings had been switched for abstract designs. The television was gone.

On the bedside table was a rosary, a Bible, and a picture of Eleanor.

"I thought you weren't Catholic anymore," I said as she wiped the lipstick off my cheek.

"Once Catholic, always Catholic. Sit on the bed," she instructed as she grabbed a hairbrush.

When she married, Emily abandoned her mother's religion for her husband's nominal faith. While she didn't seem to miss it, when I was a kid, I remember spotting her car parked at the Catholic church during confession hours on the way to the Bible-belt building I grew up going to every Sunday.

"You never said what was wrong with my hair," I reminded her as she began to brush it.

"There's nothing wrong. Except a few tangles. I just wanted an excuse to braid it. But it's getting long. Do you want me to cut it?"

"Alright. Should I wash it first?"

"No. Hold on. Let me get the scissors."

I fixed my eyes on the picture and remembered how we'd sat on the ugly wooden bed, giggling so fiercely Emily had hardly been able to keep us still for long enough to trim our hair.

Eleanor insisted she hated letting her mother do this, yet even after we went off to college in New York, she refused to have anyone else cut her hair. When I went to a salon for the first time, Eleanor claimed I'd betrayed Emily, who infuriated her daughter by complimenting the bob when she first saw it during a visit to the city.

A few months into lockdown, Hélène had cut my hair out of necessity, but not evenly. The faults were hardly noticeable to anyone except me, and by this point, they'd grown out.

"Does it bother you to see us together?" I asked as Emily set down the brush.

"I want you to be happy," she answered, pulling back a section of hair.

"That doesn't answer the question."

"No, it doesn't bother me. I like Sissy, and I love you, and I think you're good for each other. I like seeing you happy with someone."

My heart tingled until I looked at the photograph and heard Eleanor admonish me about public displays of affection.

"She never wanted you to see," I explained.

Her grip on my hair tightened. "I saw more than she thought."

"She didn't want to upset you."

"My daughter upset me constantly, but never because of love."

"It wasn't that she was worried about you judging her sexuality," I explained, "at least I don't think so. She knew you were open-minded."

"Oh, I know. She and I talked more than you think. Go take a look in the mirror."

I stood, combing my hair with my fingers. The ends were uniformly straight, cut just above where the color had started to fade. The difference was hardly visible in the mirror. Still, I could feel it as strongly as I felt Eleanor's ghost hovering behind me, poking through her mother's jewelry and lifting earrings up to her unpierced lobes and laughing about how expensive they were and what a shame it would be when she inherited them since she refused to poke holes in her body.

"Do you like it?"

"I love it," I answered, and I came back, tossing my hair over my shoulders so she could braid it.

"You've tangled it already," she tsk-ed in the way Eleanor always had.

"Sorry," I answered half-apologetically, my mind still lost amidst memories as I asked if Eleanor ever talked about us, not daring to say *me* except alongside her, for what was I without her?

Except Emily contradicted me.

"You were all she talked about. Even when you were six years old. It was Kitty this, Kitty that. Do you think Kitty will like my hair? Can Kitty come on vacation? Can Kitty live with us? Do you think Kitty likes me? Loves me?"

"Really?"

She combed back my hair, pulling strands apart and holding them so delicately I hardly felt her touch.

"Does she answer you when you pray?" I asked.

"You don't pray to people. You pray to God."

"The dead are with God."

"The saints are with God."

Eleanor was beyond the realm of mortals, but she wasn't among the saints.

"Do you think she was a sinner?" I asked.

"We're all sinners," Emily said with such conviction it sucked me back to a church pew from childhood.

"I know, but do you think she was a sinner because of us?"

"If I believed the two of you having sex was a sin, why would I have let you live with us?"

We'd had sleepovers since I was six and in high school I'd stayed for several extended periods and gone weeks without seeing my parents.

"How do you pray when God says otherwise?"

"What religion says is not necessarily what God says."

At this point, the braid was nearly complete, and I considered complaining or shaking my head so she would start over and I would have an excuse to stay.

"When you were young, I never wanted to talk about religion. I was afraid I would offend you or that your parents wouldn't let you come. But maybe I should have."

"Why?"

"I worry your parents gave you the wrong idea of God."

"And Catholicism would have given me the right one?"

"No, I don't even know if I would call myself Catholic."

"But you pray the rosary."

"I pray the rosary because my daughter is dead, and because praying through a woman whose only child died in the only way I can imagine to be more horrific than mine makes me feel like there's meaning to my life."

"Is that why I'm painting a portrait? To give your suffering meaning?"

She tied the end of the braid. "You are painting this portrait because it must be painted. For me, for you, for Sissy, for many reasons, but ultimately because you must."

"You didn't mention her."

"I'm sorry?"

"You said for you, for me, and even for Sissy, but not for her."

Emily moved the braid over my shoulder, leaning down so her lips touched my forehead and then my cheek as her arms entangled me as tenderly as I imagined an angel's embrace to be.

"No," she whispered, "I fear Eleanor is the last one we are doing this for."

Chapter Eight

L egally, Sissy's childhood ended the second a clock struck midnight, as mine had fourteen years prior, almost at the same time as Eleanor's.

Buying porn or tobacco would have been too ordinary for us back then, so would have been hosting celebrations or giving other gifts, which Emily and Thomas showered us with anyway. Eleanor never rejected the expenses her parents poured upon her. She just never embraced them, and I suspected her gifts were still unopened in boxes collecting dust.

The day I turned eighteen, I packed my belongings and left the home where I'd been born and should have been raised. My parents had expected this. They didn't protest like they had the last time Emily picked me up and announced I was staying at Rosewood indefinitely.

For most of high school I stayed at the Pontells under the excuse that it was closer to school. Initially, it had been to stay close to Eleanor and nothing more than an extended sleepover, and thinking of those days brought color to my sketches as I etched my earliest memories of Eleanor, back before she'd heard the word suicide and never would have thought to seek it out, or at least before I thought she had.

Filtering through memories, I sought answers as to when she had changed, searching scans of photos for signs of a switch.

She'd been mad as early as middle school.

I'd known that even then, but looking back upon her tween smile showed me the depths in which she'd hidden her sorrow.

While I was absorbed in reminiscence, Emily organized Sissy's dinner with a devoted dedication that didn't surprise me after re-discovering her religious rigor.

I asked Sissy if she would leave her father the day she was granted freedom, but she said she couldn't.

She had nowhere to go, though Emily made sure she knew Rosewood's doors were wide open. I overheard Emily offer one morning, but Sissy responded with excuse after excuse.

"Kitty said the same when she was in school," Emily said, and I stiffened at the sound of my name from the stairs where I hid. I hadn't told Sissy anything about my family.

"What do you mean?" Sissy asked.

"She came to stay with us. Twice. The second time was when she turned eighteen, but it was shortly before the end of her senior year, and she went off to college soon after. The first time was when she was sixteen. I kept trying to persuade her, but she kept coming up with excuses. She had siblings to take care of, and they needed help on the farm. They didn't need her help one bit."

"I don't have siblings. No one else would take care of my father."

"He's a grown man. He should be able to take care of himself."

There was a pause in the conversation, and I considered making my presence known, but Sissy spoke before I could. "What made Kitty change her mind?"

"She didn't. My husband and I drove to her house and packed her things."

"And her parents allowed it?"

"Her father had hit her. We threatened to call child services."

At this point, I retreated back upstairs, not wanting to interrupt and make the conversation more uncomfortable, and I didn't to a story I already knew, even if I was curious how Sissy might react.

I didn't see Sissy again until she arrived on her birthday. By the small size of her overnight bag, I suspected Emily's persuasions had failed. Still, Emily was no less ecstatic in her greeting, kissing Sissy's cheeks and laughing so hard she nearly cried.

"I know it's only a day, but it's strange to think of you as grown up!" Emily exclaimed, her emotions so overwhelming Sissy could hardly release herself to kiss me.

After our awkward encounter at the door, we were shy about kisses, but this one was better than most, so good that when we pulled apart, I would have brought her back to my embrace for another were Emily not insistent that we open a bottle of sparkling wine.

Sissy and I followed her into the kitchen. For the first time in a long while, I gave myself permission to celebrate and forget that my relationship with Sissy was undefined and that I still had work that needed to be finished, as Emily quickly reminded me.

She didn't mention the portrait, instead asking if I'd told Sissy about my upcoming exhibition in New York. I hadn't, which made me find an excuse as to why not.

"It's a private showing. One of these events for people who have enough money to buy overpriced art during a pandemic," I explained.

"I would remind you that you are living with one of those people," Emily chided.

"Are you going, too?" Sissy asked her.

Emily deftly popped open the bottle. "No. That's not really my kind of thing anymore. Besides, there's always so much to be done around here. I can't bring myself to leave Rosewood for very long, and not because of the pandemic."

"Why do you love it so much?"

"It's home," Emily shrugged, a sentiment so simple it was easily overseen. Rosewood was her home, and it had been for over thirty years.

Legally, it was entirely hers, but in spirit, it never would be.

Rosewood was a stately home, a historic home. To call it home was to claim its story, to erase who Emily had been born as and become permanently Pontell, to eternally embrace Eleanor.

Our glasses clinked, and we toasted to Sissy.

The conversation shifted, leaving sentimentality behind.

Sissy was working on a portfolio in preparation for college applications, and she brought several of her photographs and a short story, which I set aside to read later.

"Your work gets better and better every time I see it," Emily complimented as she spread the photographs over the counter.

"I have a good teacher."

I laughed and tried to protest, but Sissy surprised me and leaned in to peck my cheek. Heat rushed to my face, and my fingers intertwined with hers as we watched Emily flip through the images.

"The colors are magnificent. Kitty only ever does black and white."

"I like to keep things simple," I explained.

"Your art is never simple. Artists never appreciate their own work as much as others."

"And their closest friends over-appreciate their work."

"I would be lying if I said I wasn't biased." Emily set the portfolio aside and shifted her focus to the sauce simmering on the stove.

"You know, Emily," Sissy said after we'd chatted about nonsense for some time, "You said once you aren't an artist, but you're much better at understanding it than anyone I've met."

"You're sweet, but you're grown up now. You don't need to try and impress me."

"What does being grown up have to do with it? Kitty tries to impress you all the time."

I laughed and sipped my wine so quickly that the bubbles caught in my throat.

"No, she knows she doesn't need to impress me. I think she's trying to impress you." Emily gave Sissy a suggestive look that made me sip even more quickly.

That eighteen years but not seventeen years and three hundred and sixty-four days enabled Sissy to consent was ridiculous. The very existence of such laws sent my thoughts soaring to subversive sexuality that I suppressed with more sips of sparkles. The conversation turned, as it would many times throughout the night, but my thoughts always returned to Sissy.

The later the night went on, the more complicated it became to force myself to stop fantasizing what it would be like to undress her down to her underwear, to kiss her in spots she didn't know she wanted to be touched so that she might touch me in ways I knew I wanted to be loved.

"Eleanor was no artist."

Her name brought me back to reality, shaming me for becoming so lost in fantasy I didn't realize Emily had begun to speak of her, as she only did when necessary or when she could no longer confine her sorrow to the constraints of herself.

We'd finished dessert and exhausted more topics than I could count, but my stomach churned sour as I realized I hadn't been listening for the past half hour.

"She wanted to be," Emily continued, sharing more than I'd heard in seven years. "Maybe she felt she couldn't. We never pushed her with responsibilities, but they're impossible to escape in a place like this, especially as an only child. I wish I'd had more children. Not because she wasn't enough. She was more than enough. Too much, even." She wasn't so drunk that her words slurred, but they would start to before long. "But if I'd had more children, maybe she would have felt less alone. I was alone growing up."

She sipped her wine. We'd moved on to red, and at this point, the meal had nearly finished, and I hardly noticed how much Emily had drunk, starting to feel the effects myself.

"She wasn't alone," I reassured her, "she had you."

"She had you more than she had me."

"And I had five siblings and always felt alone. Except when I was with her."

It wasn't entirely true.

With Eleanor, I could feel more alone than I had been in lockdown. But when she didn't make me feel so alone that I barely felt human, she had made me feel more alive than a crowd speaking in tongues, so ecstatic I couldn't conceive a sensation such as loneliness had ever haunted my heart, not when there was overwhelming and intoxicating ecstasy so profound it couldn't exist except through Eleanor.

"It's getting late, and I'm getting old," Emily sighed, standing and taking her plate to the sink. Sissy offered to help clean, and Emily laughed, shaking her head as she came back to us, leaning over to wrap her arms around Sissy and kiss her head. "I'll clean up tomorrow and give you your gift."

"I said not to get me anything!"

Emily kissed her again and then me, running her fingers through the length of my hair, twirling the edges at the tips of her fingers, possessing a look that was full of maternal affection yet so full of secrets it made me wish my hair were lighter like Eleanor's so that she might love it more.

Then she left, and Sissy and I were alone as adults, except there was nothing grown up about the childish way my heart was skipping beats.

We sat for some time in silence, unable to address that Eleanor had been spoken of or that Sissy was suddenly considered sexually mature.

When we spoke, we weren't really speaking, only talking, creating a small talk preface for the moment when we would stand in front of my door and dance around what the sequel to that first kiss might be.

I said I was tired, so we went upstairs, and at the door, we didn't kiss.

Instead, she came to my room and, after rushed kisses and awkward removing of shoes, to my bed.

Clothes couldn't be torn away quickly enough. Still, we couldn't bring ourselves to further steps until she reached underneath my underwear and froze as though surprised at what she'd found.

I stroked her hair, bringing her close for a kiss, and was about to ask if she was alright, except she moved her fingers. My eyes closed, and I was unable to see, much less speak.

"Do you like it?" she asked, and I couldn't respond except by taking her face in my hands and kissing her so fiercely she stopped. We kept kissing, and when I thought she was ready, I began to touch her.

She shivered, grabbing hold of my arms.

I kept going, and her grip tightened, her face contorting. At first, I thought in pleasure, but then I saw it was fear, and my fingers froze.

I wrapped my arms around her, kissing her hair as her head fell onto my shoulders. "I'm sorry," I whispered.

"I'm sorry," she managed through tears, "I'm not ready."

"That's nothing to be sorry for."

"Are you upset?"

"Of course not!" I looked her in the eyes and made sure she knew I meant it when I said, "never feel like you have to do anything you don't want to."

She cried, and we crawled under the sheets together. She cuddled close to me, and I remembered just how young she was.

"Happy birthday," I whispered, but she had already fallen asleep.

CHAPTER NINE

Touch is most sore when fresh.

Days apart from Sissy were years within my skin. Each and every mile between Rosewood and Manhattan was felt when I went to bed without her. My muscles missed the presence of her weight pressing mine, fighting the burning in my body for Eleanor that passed whenever I walked past a park where we'd picnicked, a café where we'd kissed, a building she'd nearly jumped off of.

Twice, she'd threatened to kill herself in front of me, once when we were in school and another during college.

It was one of the many weekends when Emily visited. She'd often come to take her mind off of her divorce, not realizing how much her doing so irritated her daughter.

Something during our decadent lunch set Eleanor off, and she ran through the fire escape up to the rooftop.

It was insane. Her mother hadn't said anything too upsetting, but Eleanor's reaction hadn't surprised me. The memory was still numb, and when I walked by the skyscraper, it wasn't the first thing that came to mind.

Of all things, I thought of the salmon they'd served, of how sad I'd been when I learned smoked salmon meant cold salmon.

I snapped a photo of the building and when I entered my hotel room, I sketched Eleanor as I remembered her here.

In the four years we'd lived in New York, we'd grown from angsty teenagers into eager adults.

I'd studied journalism even though I couldn't write well and knew art was my calling.

Eleanor pursued philosophy and pre-law, searching for meaning she knew she would never find.

Every night, we'd stay up in our dorm, musing over marijuana and margaritas and our latest museum trip.

We visited an exhibition nearly every week and a show almost every other. Culture was the reason we'd left our dull little down, except even in the mess of Manhattan, Eleanor carried Rosewood with her. She knew her place among skyscrapers was temporary, and in spite of her dedication to her home, or perhaps because of it, she commanded the streets as though they were hers, her identity too specific to be molded into Manhattan manners.

Though the city's anonymity startled me when we first arrived, I came to thrive in its busyness so well that its emptiness during this lockdown-era visit unsettled me.

The streets were not as desolate as those of Vienna had been at the beginning of the pandemic, but without its beat, New York was not the city Eleanor and I had lived in.

I wasn't staying far from the building she'd nearly jumped from, and from my hotel, I hardly recognized it. At first, I recognized nothing except the prominent landmarks.

My hotel was close to the gallery, a convenient location for rich art customers. It was also the part of town the Pontells had always stayed in.

They traveled extensively as soon as we went off to college, spoiling us whenever they'd come to the city, taking us to soirees and introducing us to the society that was too snooty for Texans but accepted the Pontells because they were richer and came from families older than their own.

Thomas and Emily's aim wasn't to secure a husband for Eleanor, but everyone interpreted it as such, and the Upper East Side jerks were intent on scoring their exotic Pontell prize.

Eleanor never said she was with me when we went to these parties, and I never said I was with her in any way except the way friends always attended events together. We never said we were with one another to each other, but when I slept with one of those boys...

well ...

She threatened to jump off the building across from him.

I stopped in my tracks, not in front of the building, but at the crosswalk that led to the side of town where I'd first had sex with a boy.

He had been my first, and I wish he'd been my only and that the first time with him had been the last.

The building was blocks away, but I couldn't even turn in its direction.

I returned to my hotel room and began to draw as soon as the door shut.

I didn't even see what I drew until I came back from the exhibition that evening.

My agent had nearly been forced to drag me out of the room, and throughout the night, she kept reminding me I had to smile and say nice things to the people willing to pay thousands for my paintings.

Some of them knew the Pontells, many of them had met Lana Lane at least once, and all of them knew about Eleanor.

Everyone did.

She'd been written into the blurb that some intern had written for the event, a fact that my agent apologized profusely for and that I ignored by ordering more espresso.

Most of them had probably seen the sex tape. I wasn't as sensitive about it as Eleanor, so I forced smiles when Lana was mentioned. She was filming another movie. The film was all hush-hush, so they only mentioned it in false whispers.

I couldn't leave quickly enough.

I should have stayed and chit-chatted more, but it became late enough that tiredness was a valid excuse for departure, and I returned to drawing.

Dawn came, and I had hardly moved from my seat.

If my flight hadn't been soon, I wouldn't have moved for hours.

Reality was like a dream, as though I were rewatching someone who looked like me driving to the airport, taking her shoes off at security, and buckling a seatbelt as loosely as possible.

As soon as the airplane gate closed, my head slumped against the window.

My last image of New York was a runway. I don't remember anything between that and Emily waiting at baggage claim, except for my dream, Eleanor.

My dream was not visceral, only sweet. It was as though she knew the discomfort I felt in my confined airline space. I wanted to escape onto her spacious balcony overlooking the endless horizon of Rosewood, and collapse into arms that I believed could hold me for eternity.

That was right after we'd graduated college, and everything about her room seemed small.

She told me Rosewood seemed small, and after four years in a dorm, I couldn't agree, but I understood.

Everything was too small for Eleanor, including me.

She should have been the one to go abroad, and she did, but only to visit me during my foreign residencies.

She was disappointed in Rome, not because the pasta wasn't cooked the way it was in America or because the Colosseum wasn't as impressive as on television, but because of the man's sweater hidden in the back of my closet and the condoms at the bottom of the drawer.

I wondered if Emily had heard about that, if Eleanor had ever cried on her shoulder with a broken heart.

I was glad that it was so hard to talk with a mask on because if it weren't, I would have poured everything out in the instant I saw Emily waving at baggage claim.

By the time we reached the car, I'd composed myself enough for a decent conversation.

"This was Thomas's car," I noted as I tossed my bag in the trunk. I'd been in the garage a few times, so I knew it was still there alongside the truck and the empty space where Eleanor's convertible had been.

"Didn't want the engine to get rusty," Emily answered.

"Or you just like driving a sports car."

It was the kind of car that made your mouth water just thinking about it.

"I actually don't, but I thought you might like being picked up in it."

Eleanor would have been upset if her mother had picked her up with anything less expensive.

"How's Sissy?" I asked, trying to hide my disappointment that she wasn't there, but I hadn't asked her to meet me, so I shouldn't have expected it.

"I wouldn't know. I haven't seen her all week. I took her to school shopping over the weekend but haven't heard from her since then."

"School shopping?" I asked skeptically.

"She still has a year of high school."

"I know, but it's online."

"I know, and her computer is about as old as she is."

"You bought her a computer?"

"A laptop."

"She let you do that?" I would have thought Sissy's pride prevented her from accepting such an expensive gift.

"Yup."

"Where can you even buy a laptop in town?"

"Nowhere. We drove to Austin."

"You took my girlfriend to Austin and bought her a laptop?"

"Is she your girlfriend?" Emily raised an eyebrow as she fired up the engine. "I bought her some clothes too. And lunch. I couldn't stand that flowery dress anymore."

"I like that dress."

"Of course you do. It's too tight."

"What's wrong with women wearing tight clothes?"

"Nothing, except she's eighteen and no one has bought her clothes since she was fourteen." Emily's grip on the wheel tightened, and I looked out the window, trying to remember what the road had looked like before fast food chains popped up. "You didn't answer my question," she said after we'd passed a few exits.

"Which question?"

"If she's your girlfriend or not."

"Does it matter?"

"The girl's practically living at my house."

"I lived at your house when I was her age and you never asked about my relationship status."

"You lived at my house because your father beat you, not because you were sleeping with my daughter, and I asked her about your relationship many times."

"What did she say?" I shifted in my seat, my heart pounding as I prepared for the worst, but Emily clicked on the blinker, pausing as she waited to shift lanes, as though she needed to be polite in a car like this.

"It was complicated. You were both young and in love."

We'd always been in love, and Eleanor would always be young.

Emily and I passed several exits before she continued in a softer tone, "Sweetheart, I only have space in my heart for so much heartbreak. I care about Sissy, and I don't want to see her go. I know she'll grow up and go off to college, but if she's just some fling for you, I need to know."

"She's not," I insisted.

"Good."

She seemed content to leave it at that, but I needed to explain.

"I haven't felt this way about anyone before. Not with Hélène," I said quickly, "Not even with Lana. With Lana it was completely different. I'll never have that again, but with Sissy … I don't know. I can't describe it."

I didn't dare compare what I felt for Sissy with how I'd felt for Eleanor. It wouldn't have been fair to either of them.

We approached the exit for the town, and I was tempted to pull out my phone and invite Sissy over. It was Saturday, so she didn't have school, but I stopped myself, knowing Emily would glare at me for using my phone and because Sissy knew I was flying back today.

If Sissy wanted to see me, she would come.

Besides, my mind was still absorbed with Eleanor.

My drawings were evolving in my head as I played out the four years we'd lived in New York.

"It's sweet. Seeing you in love. It makes me feel young again."

We were on the state highway now, and before too long, Rosewood would be in sight.

"Have you loved anyone? Since Thomas?" I asked.

"I've had plenty of lovers, but no. I haven't fallen in love with anyone. I don't want to, either. I'm happy with what I have, especially with you here."

I wondered if the day would ever come when I would feel the same, or if I would always be searching to fill Eleanor's absence, or if I could even recognize contentment if it came.

"How'd the show go by the way?" Emily asked as we turned onto the road for Rosewood.

"The art sold well."

"Did you enjoy it?"

"I never enjoy those things."

"Did you at least enjoy New York?"

The gates to the ranch opened as we approached, the iron creaking at the hinges. My heart beat fast as the house rose over the horizon.

"It's good to be home," I answered, unable to admit that though my body had traveled to New York, my mind had visited a version of Eleanor, who had been a stranger to her mother for four years.

When we went in, Emily asked if I was hungry.

I hadn't eaten anything all day, but I said no.

I needed to paint.

CHAPTER TEN

L ife is nothing but a rough draft for art.

Eleanor told me that, although she'd said it personally as opposed to poetically.

I'd been so absorbed by painting I hardly heard her.

Only later was I struck by those words, after it was too late to realize she'd said them in anger.

It was in London, less than a year after we graduated college. I was living there for an internship, which delayed my plans to return to Texas for another half-year.

At twenty-three, that meant half a lifetime, and half a year in London led to another half in Paris and then more and more halves in more cities and in less time so that it might as well have been like kissing Eleanor goodbye.

She visited when she could, and when she said those words, she was posing in preparation for a multimedia exhibit I was preparing.

After returning to Rosewood from the show in Manhattan, I pulled out the images for the first time since I'd taken them in London. They'd never been put on display. Eleanor wouldn't allow it even though she hadn't seen them.

She was a year into law school, but there was no evidence of all-nighters or stress despite her perfect grades and busy schedule, just as there were no signs of a daughter whose parents had just finalized their divorce or a lover whose relationship was falling apart.

Instead, there was a bright young woman mature beyond her years but girlish in her gaze, possessing the power of a princess and the beauty of a goddess who, for some reason, was in love with an unworthy me.

In a painting, she could be any woman I wanted her to be, even the woman she wanted to be.

I tried to paint the woman I remembered, but her eyes eluded me as she lifted her body, suggesting the move she was about to make.

She would reach her hand under my shirt, resting her hand on the expensive lingerie she'd bought me.

For a while, she didn't say anything, and I continued painting.

Motionless, she kept her hand wrapped around my breast, waiting for me to respond as though every nerve in my body were not fighting the urge to thrust my brush aside and take her in my arms.

Art overpowered her, and though the anger in her words seeped through, in that instant, I was too intent on capturing that which could never be caught, thus losing her forever.

I wouldn't have thought it; given the sex we had once, I eventually tossed the brush aside.

Eleanor could be rough and always possessive.

When making love to her, there was no room for wandering thoughts or fantasy.

She tore the lingerie with her teeth, biting me so hard I thought I would scream.

In the photograph, the mischief in her eyes suggested premeditation. I never would have seen it without my memories, except Emily saw something.

She'd never seen the images before, and she rarely entered my studio, but I'd been cooped up for nearly two days.

She didn't urge me to stop or leave but brought food and opened a window, feeling my forehead to ensure I wasn't feverish, which is how I must have looked.

"Sissy says she's sick," she said once I'd started nibbling on my sandwich. It struck me that I hadn't looked at my phone or even thought much of the lover who was infinitely more alive than the one on canvas.

"With what?" I asked, my face flushing as Emily's gaze wandered to my work.

Quickly, I promised that Eleanor's portrait wouldn't be a nude.

"She was naked when I gave birth to her." Emily noted as though it was not a strange segue from Sissy's illness. She picked up one of the photographs, "Even here I see her the day she was born. Seven pounds, nine ounces. Ten toes, ten fingers. I counted. Just to be sure. She didn't cry, not even a little. She wasn't asleep, just silent. The doctor was afraid something was wrong, but I knew she was fine, or at least I thought so. She was sadder than I knew."

"I don't think babies can be sad."

"They say birth is traumatic."

"Is it?"

"I don't remember being born," Emily laughed, reaching for the other photos, "but giving birth is."

I swallowed a bite of my sandwich, and she nodded to the water, interjecting a warning about dehydration. "Does it hurt?" I asked.

"Dehydration?"

"Giving birth."

She sat down, flipping from one photograph to the next. The prints were glossy, the background dark against Emily's pale skin while high-lighting the smoothness of her even paler, polished fingernails.

"It's the second most agonizing thing I've felt in my life."

My spine tingled, the memory of Eleanor's sharp nails scratching my vertebrae through the lingerie, the iciness of her hands hardening the nerves around my nipples, nearly gasping as Emily ran her hand over the image before tossing it with less reverence than a mother should have held for the sole record of her daughter's body at the prime of beauty.

"Did you give birth naturally?" I asked.

Emily nodded as she looked around at the pieces of art scattered around the room. "I wanted a c-section, but she had other plans. She came out quickly, though. I suppose I should be thankful for that."

As though a woman should have been thankful for experiencing less pain rather than more.

"Did you plan to have her?"

"You mean was she an accident?"

Emily was so honest about sex that I knew more than I had the right to about her experiences, but she'd told me little about her marital relations. They'd married young, and Eleanor followed shortly after, although not seen enough to suggest anything indecent by small-town standards.

"I suppose so. We planned on having children, but not so soon."

"Did you want more?"

I could see from the wringing of her hands how much the questions hurt, but her pain proved the necessity of the answers.

"At first, yes. We said we would wait, but time kept ticking and eventually we ran out of it. Or I did. But it didn't matter. She was enough."

Her voice caught, and she struggled to continue.

"Thomas wanted another baby after she died. Even though we were divorced and I was nearly fifty. I couldn't even think about it. The thought of having another child just makes me sick. She was mine, and she was everything I ever wanted, all I ever wanted."

Here she was, unfolding her heart like I'd wanted, and all I thought was what a shame it was I wasn't recording so I could watch it later in hopes of capturing the sentiment in my portrait.

"But she was infuriating. She drove me so mad there were times I wanted to hurt her, but I wouldn't have wanted any other daughter, or any other child. – She was perfect, and I loved her. I still love her. – I love her so much I wish I didn't, because most days I wake up and think

I'd be better off shooting myself in that stupid barn that I can't even persuade myself to bulldoze."

I looked out the window. Before too long, the barn wouldn't need bulldozing. The wood would collapse of its own accord, and all that would be left of the final sight Eleanor had seen would be sawdust.

"She deserved a better mother than me. Any other mother would have seen how dark her suffering was. I saw some, but I didn't do enough. If she had another mother, she might still be here, and even though I wouldn't know her then, she might not be dead and -"

I took her hands.

Trembling, she stroked my hair, her words giving way to wails as I rested my head in her lap.

I wept, too, but silently. This was her time for her grief, and her sorrow demanded the suppression of mine.

"From the second I saw you, I wanted you to be my mother," I admitted

She combed her fingers through my hair. "If I'd given birth to you, I couldn't love you the way I do. In some ways you are as much a daughter to me as she was."

And in other ways, not at all, I thought, but instead said, "She resented it."

"She brought that upon herself. It wasn't fair, the way she loved you."

I shivered, wondering what Emily saw in those pictures and what secrets of mine and Eleanor's weren't secrets at all.

"I should have stopped it," she said.

"We loved each other."

"Neither of you knew how to love."

"I love her. I would do anything for her. So would you."

"I'm her mother."

"I'm her lover."

"You were her lover."

My mouth opened without making a sound.

"Sissy is your lover now, and something with her isn't right. If you don't go to her, how are you loving her any less wrongly than the way Eleanor loved you?"

CHAPTER ELEVEN

The Evergreen property was lined by a rusting chicken-wire fence with signs warning against trespassing. The gate was so shoddy it couldn't have even kept a chicken out.

Before it was in sight, barking anticipated my arrival at a house half-sunken into dust and disappearing under overgrown bushes and creeping woods, lost in a lawn littered with foldable furniture and torn chew toys.

As I shut off the engine, a man swung open the house's inner door, standing safely behind a screen, failing to keep out the flies for which it was meant.

Even from the porch steps, he reeked of whiskey.

"Hello, Mr. Evergreen. My name is-"

"Sign said no trespassing."

The floorboards creaked under my weight. "I know, but-"

"Can't ya read?"

"Of course, but," I sighed and quit with the small talk neither of us wanted to have. "I'm here to see Sissy."

Danny Evergreen must have been about Emily's age, but his weight and sunken eyes added another ten years. From what I'd heard, he hadn't always been a drunk, but of course, no one began life as an alcoholic.

"Girl's sick," he spat.

"I know. That's why I'm here. I brought some soup," I explained with the sweetest smile I could conjure as I slipped into my Texan tongue as best I could after years as an outsider.

"Don't you liberals say we ought not keep our distance due to this pandemic?"

I clenched my teeth into a tight smile. "Could I at least see her through the door?"

"She's asleep. Shoulda called first."

"I did call. Several times. It's why I'm here. There was no answer, so I got worried."

"Can't ya take a hint? Maybe she don't like you anymore."

"Maybe I could wait until she wakes up? And then we could let Sissy decide?"

From another room, I heard a voice. Though muffled by moldy walls, I recognized it instantly. The words were indistinct, but from her father's tone as he hollered over his shoulder, it was clear he didn't want them heard.

Seizing the chance, I thrust through the screen door, shoving him aside and sending the hinges rattling.

"Hey! Get outta my house!" He swore as I stormed through and struggled not to trip over miscellaneous scatterings of beer bottles and tobacco trays, ignoring the posters of half-naked women and confederate flags.

Despite the peeling wallpaper, stepping into Sissy's room was like entering a world so separate from the roach-infested rest I scarcely believed it existed.

The windows were open, and the air was scented with half-burnt candles. They were cheap candles, but even ordinary oxygen would have smelled nice compared with the swamp in the hall.

Then I saw Sissy.

In her eyes, I found the girl I had long wanted to save, her lips tremoring as tears struggled to escape eyes from which the reflection was fractured: the savior I had dreamed of but never found, the lover who freed me from lust while withholding love.

Then there was me.

And behind those eyes was a girl with a black eye and bruised arms.

Inside of me, a little girl squirmed, my stomach twisting as Emily threw open my suitcases and started packing. It wasn't until I heard Thomas arguing with my parents that I summoned the courage to help.

Before me, Sissy rushed to cover the marks and excuse the bruises.

So, I did what Eleanor should have done and followed her mother's lead.

Sissy was not as confident as I had been, sobbing and shrinking into a corner so small I feared frightening her with my command to go to the car. She flinched, and later in therapy, I regretted my harsh tone, but in less than five minutes, Sissy was moving out.

I asked if there was anything I should be sure to grab.

"I don't want anything from this house," she managed.

"Then get your artwork and your schoolwork."

On the porch, I pulled out my wallet, silencing her father's shouts as his bloodshot eyes began to glisten and bills fresh from the brank shuffled through my fingers.

I shoved the money into his sweaty hands as quickly as I could. "If you come near her again, I'll call the police, though I should anyway after seeing her face."

He thumbed the edges of the bills, crumpling their crisp corners. "Most of it is that boyfriend's handiwork."

My lips twisted. "Boyfriend?"

"That upset you, huh? She went to see him last weekend and came back with that black eye. Maybe he figured something out. Everyone around here knows what kind of stuff you like. It's even on video." He smirked and then spat over the side of the porch. My spine cringed at the thought of this stinking excuse for a man having seen my nude body on a screen alongside one as pristine as Lana Lane's. "Now, get off my property and go back to that haunted ranch of yours, dike pervert."

It was only a few miles to Rosewood, but with every one that we passed, I admired Sissy more and more for her long walks and bike rides in such conditions and in such heat.

She slumped into the passenger seat, refusing to look at me.

The accusation about a boyfriend burned in my mind, but I couldn't burden her with jealousy when we'd never claimed exclusivity, and even so, she didn't deserve more suffering.

As Rosewood rose over the horizon, she flipped down the blind to look at her black eye in the mirror. She opened the glove compartment and then asked to see my purse.

"Emily would see through makeup," I told her as I clicked the button for the gate. Besides, I didn't have any.

She flipped up the blind and sunk back into the seat. "I'm sorry," she said so quietly I hardly heard.

I sighed, wondering what I would have wanted Eleanor to say if she'd saved me, but all I remembered was how Emily had held me as I wept.

When I parked, I held out my hand. She rested hers in it, and I leaned forward to brush away a tear as lightly as I could.

She shivered and shed another tear.

"May I kiss you?" I asked.

She nodded.

My lips only brushed hers out of fear of shattering the bruises on her face, but she returned it with more force than I expected, breaking the rhythm of my beating heart.

After that moment, it never beat the same again, though it was not me who comforted Sissy in the tender hours to follow.

As she had with me years ago, Emily embraced Sissy and welcomed her home, drawing her a bath and tucking her into bed.

It was a mother's love the girl needed, not a lover's.

She would sleep long. She needed rest.

And I needed to draw.

But that night, I couldn't enter my studio.

Eleanor was in my studio, and I wanted to be with Sissy, but I knew better than to disrupt her rest.

I considered waking Emily, but we shared a whiskey, and for now, that would have to suffice.

Emily only had so much energy, and after she'd poured out so much of her soul the night before, that didn't leave much room for me when Sissy required so much.

She asked, though, if I needed her.

As always, her offer was sincere and held the fullness of her heart, which is why I said no, and when she didn't believe me and tried to stay by my side, I changed my answer to yes, I did need her, but not now.

I spent that night without even the company of dreams. At some stage, I might have slept, but by the morning, I wasn't sure if the whole day had been a dream or a fantasy.

Sissy wasn't at breakfast, and Emily hadn't cooked, only fixed herself a coffee. Her newspaper sat unopened on the table.

I kissed her cheek before making my cappuccino. She didn't react until I sat across from her several minutes later.

She said Sissy wanted to see me.

She didn't offer more words. Once her coffee was empty and she saw I didn't need her, she announced she was going to get a head start to the day. There were countless tasks on the ranch, but none that really needed her, not when she paid people to do them.

Judging by the bags under her eyes, she had slept worse than I had.

She kissed the top of my head on her way out, leaving the space of her lips indented on my unbrushed hair.

I chose to leave it when I went to see Sissy.

She was sound asleep, so I pulled a chair up beside her bed, tempted to sketch her and preserve this broken beauty, but her beauty wasn't mine to claim.

It was hours before she woke, and I'd dozed off in the chair. I jumped at her first stirrings.

There was no tiredness in her voice. She did not request breakfast, asked no questions. All she wanted was a bath.

I prepared it.

"Stay," she insisted once the water was warm.

I averted my eyes as she dropped her towel to the ground, keeping my gaze fixed on the tiles as I sat at the edge as she requested.

She let her body adjust to the temperature, and the parts of her that weren't black and blue warmed to pink the longer she soaked in the tub.

I leaned my head back against the wall, inhaling the scents of salts so sweet I had to smile, though as soon as my lips curved up, I thought there was nothing to smile about.

"Would you like a duck?" I asked, offering her one from the side of the tub.

She swirled the rubber animal over the surface and ducked it under, bloating its tummy with water and then pointing it to my face. I squeezed my eyes shut, giggling as the water squirted my cheeks.

"Would you like a towel?" she teased, mimicking my tone and tickling my nose with a hand towel, but it dropped between our fingers into the water, and I had to fetch another.

As I wiped my face, she drew her legs into her chest, resting her head against her knees. She turned her face away from me to the tiles, admitting, "I did something I shouldn't have."

"Whatever you did," I said, "you don't deserve to get hit."

She turned her head over so her other cheek pressed against her knees, highlighting the bruises around her eyes as they flickered towards me. "I did something I shouldn't have done to you."

"I would never hit you," I reassured her, pulling myself closer and resting a hand on the top of her hair. She'd tied it up in a bun, revealing the purple marks around the edge of her face. "Even if you would want this – if you want us to stop, I wouldn't hurt you. I couldn't."

"I do want you!"

Her neck rose, and she lifted wet fingers to flick away tears, but even the gentle touch hurt and she winced. I scooted closer but pulled my hand away from her head, covering my mouth while suppressing a storm swelling in my stomach.

"But I had to be sure," she explained as her eyes welled with more water, "And I've known Jack so long it's like he has this hold over me. It was a mistake. Such a stupid, terrible mistake!"

"It wasn't a mistake. It was his mistake." My hands shook as I leaned closer to her face. "I'll kill him, and your father, too. Well, maybe not kill, but take care of them."

"No," she insisted.

"They should be in jail!"

"I think I'd prefer to let my father drink himself to death. He probably will with all the money you gave him. He couldn't do that in jail."

I shouldn't have laughed, but I did.

"And Jack..." she shook her head. "His father's the county sheriff."

"Shit."

I ran my fingers over my forehead and over my face, rubbing my temples before finally nodding in assent.

This was her decision.

"Will you photograph me?"

I lowered my hands, wrapping my arms around my legs. I hadn't photographed any living being since Eleanor, not even a fish, but I didn't need to think to answer.

"Yeah."

"Tonight. Before the bruises fade."

I swallowed, struggling to nod. "Alright."

That night, Sissy came to my room, where I'd already set up the equipment, and averted my eyes as Sissy undressed.

Once she was nude, I snapped a few shots without really looking.

Lowering the camera, I crossed my arms as I watched her try to find how she preferred to sit. She struggled with the sheets, raising and dropping them as she decided how much she wanted to be covered.

The urge to touch burned under my fingertips and the quiet clicks of the lens satiated my desire as best they could as I was careful to keep control over the desperation to soothe her with my skin and the urge to capture her image in a way other than which she desired.

Though it had been years since a model had sat for me, the process returned as naturally as driving down a familiar road, albeit with newfound delicacy.

Eleanor had always been brazenly unabashed, provoking me to take photos I didn't want to take, so snapping without warning had become my standard.

With Sissy, that wasn't an option. Whenever she seemed uneasy, I stopped, pretending to change a setting on the camera while she settled into a more comfortable position.

I didn't have the equipment I would have liked for a portrait photo-shoot, but this wasn't about capturing candid shots.

These would never be sold, and once printed, they would stay shield-ed from any eyes but ours, or even from any except hers, if that's what she wished.

I closed my eyes, trying to give her some privacy. When I opened my eyes and found she'd hidden nothing, I understood her desire for exposure.

I lifted my camera and clicked the shutter, and then I moved closer, drawing myself deeper into the scene with every click. Gradually, the barriers between art and love dropped as I crawled into the bed. Running one hand over her body while the other held the camera, I felt her muscles tensing, and my touch softened.

Supporting her head, I drew it up closer to the camera, snapping shots of her face as I turned her cheeks from side to side, tracing the outlines of her bruises with my thumb before bringing her head to my lips as I ran my lips so I could run them over the dark marks. Then I rested her head back on the pillow, lifting the camera to my eye while my hand skimmed over her neck and breasts and then her stomach, stopping between her legs.

She was wet.

Yanking my hand away, I jerked the camera back, looking as far away from her as I could.

"I'm sorry. I'll stop."

"No."

She seized my hand, pulling it back to where it had been.

I gasped, trying to pull away.

"I need you to touch me."

Her grip softened, and my chest heaved a heavy breath while I loosened my fingers.

She lifted her head from the pillow, releasing a light, pleasurable gasp.

"Don't stop," she whined, and when I lowered my camera, she strained her neck, saying, "No. I meant the photos."

My fingers stopped, my face twisting as I shook my head. "I don't make-" I began without finishing, unable to bring myself to say the word porn since I knew that wasn't how she viewed this, and depending on how one interpreted the video I'd made with Lena, that wasn't exactly true.

She pulled herself up, bringing her hands around my neck as she tugged my neck down for a kiss.

"Please. I need you to." As her lips pulled back, she dropped her hands to my shoulders, resting her forehead against mine. "Make art of recovery, not damage."

I swallowed, nodding in consent as she lay her head back down. I lifted my camera up to my eye, beginning again to touch her. Before she could come, I switched off the camera, leaning back to set it beside the bed.

She tried to argue, but on this point, I wouldn't budge.

"Some pieces are better left unfinished," I explained.

Her face twisted in dissatisfaction, and I touched her again.

"Don't worry," I reassured her. "Only some things."

CHAPTER TWELVE

B ombarded with the aromas of sizzling, simmering spices, my mind tasted Sissy's kiss before my tongue did, sucking salt from a second helping of her tongue until she severed the sensation to return to the stove.

I tugged at the strings of her apron, saying she looked cute in it.

Emily laughed from the other side of the kitchen, saying she hadn't thought I was the sort who wanted a housewife.

"I didn't think I did, either," I teased as I leaned over Sissy's shoulder to see what was cooking.

"Emily's teaching me to make gumbo," Sissy explained.

I'd been gone all day after driving to Austin to pick up the sample prints of my magazine.

Nearly two months had passed since Sissy had moved in.

She had opted to attend her senior year online, and I spent most of my days in my studio. Emily was always busy with tasks around the ranch, so none of us ever left Rosewood except for the occasional grocery trip.

Given the property's size, we never felt confined, but our bodies constricted themselves to patterns.

I jogged, the three of us had breakfast, and then I worked. Sissy had class, Emily did some sort of manual labor, and before the end of the day, we found each other again at supper, which Emily, despite being the busiest of us, always cooked.

Sissy had put on some weight since she'd arrived. She wasn't walking home as she had before and sat in front of a computer all day. The weight wasn't much, and I wouldn't have noticed had we not continued our nightly photoshoots.

She wanted a record of her recovery, or so she claimed. It turned her on to be seen through a lens, even if I only snapped a single shot before we started tearing off each other's clothes.

The pictures remained unprinted and unseen, and we hadn't discussed when we would look at them or if we ever would.

The process was a pleasure, not the product.

As I watched her stir the gumbo, I fantasized of a home of our own, one in which I could sprawl her over the counter and kiss her when and wherever I wanted, with or without my camera.

Emily didn't mind our affection, and I didn't care if she saw, but this was her home and there were boundaries not to be crossed.

"How does the magazine look?" Emily asked.

I pulled the copies out of my bag. Sissy picked one up and flipped through the thick, shiny pages. I'd read it several times, but seeing her fingers tracing the print breathed life into the text, sending my blood pumping hot as I awaited her approval.

After glancing over the headlines and gazing over the most intriguing images, she turned to the table of contents and the letter from the editor.

"You look too posed," she noted about my tiny headshot.

"It is posed. It's a professional photograph," I countered, but I knew she was right. I was uncomfortable on the other side of the camera, and I purposely hadn't asked a great or even good photographer to take it.

She began reading aloud as Emily took back control of the cooking.

"You know I don't need you to read it," I murmured. "I wrote it."

"I know, and I edited it."

"So strongly you shouldn't have to read it."

I didn't like writing. I wasn't good, though I wasn't bad in the sense that there were usually no errors in my text. Still, I submitted to Sissy's request and permitted her to perfect my phrasing.

"Well, I haven't read it," Emily interrupted, switching the magazine for a spoon.

While she read silently, I asked Sissy about school.

Usually, she would have been at the point in the semester when she needed to cram for exams, but it didn't seem the teachers or students took online classes seriously, and she was a senior, which meant she didn't need to do much anyway. She mentioned an essay and a book she had to read, but I was only half-listening.

The aromas were impossible to ignore as I anticipated Emily's judgment on my magazine.

"How are the college essays going?" Emily asked, and I twitched at the fact that this conversation with Sissy was more interesting than the publication I'd devoted hours to.

I didn't hear Sissy's answer, or I forgot it as soon as I did.

The colors on the cover were brighter than they'd appeared on my screen, so the contrast was more significant, which wasn't what I had wanted.

I picked up a copy and turned it over. The barcode covered too much, and the price distracted from important text. My name was too big, standing out too much with the bright colors and bold font.

The works were good. There was only one piece I hadn't wanted to include, but it fit in better with the print copy than I'd feared, though I still thought it needed improvement.

There were no typos, and aside from the cover, the colors came out well. In one of the photographs the proportions had been altered in printing, albeit so minutely I doubted even the artist would notice.

"Should we open Champagne? To celebrate the magazine?"

"Sure," I answered, refraining from pointing out that Emily had hardly even looked at it.

When we sat for supper, Sissy and I sat at either side with Emily at the head.

In the old days, when we'd eaten in the dining room instead of the kitchen, Eleanor and I sat opposite Emily and Thomas, or more often only opposite Emily since Thomas was frequently away on business.

Eleanor and her mother argued at every meal, ordinarily about the most insignificant subjects.

To compensate, I had always been overly polite.

At my family's table, my father and brothers discussed men's matters, and I was the usual butt of a joke because of my artistic interests and avant-garde ideas, so I remained silent out of fear. My mother and sisters did the same, yet still, I held hatred in my heart for the fact that they stayed, for the fact that their staying forced me to stay, for the fact that my family could have looked like the Pontells but didn't and couldn't because no family looked like the Pontells.

The popping of a Champagne cork would have been met with cries of Satanism, I thought as our flutes clinked. Though I met Emily and Sissy's gazes during our little toast, I eyed the magazine from the corner of my gaze.

My family was sober, stonely so.

The cover alone would have given my parents cause to disown me.

Emily kissed my cheek and congratulated me. Sissy kissed my lips and adored me. Eleanor couldn't kiss me.

I sipped the Champagne and all night, I sipped and listened to chatter, chiming in enough so that they knew I was at least half-listening.

The two of them would make for an excellent portrait.

The mother without a daughter and daughter without a mother, like the medieval paintings of saints, women who chose the family of the church while rejecting or running from their own, women painted as virgins even if they weren't.

An icon, almost.

It never would have occurred to me to paint an icon of Eleanor, except I saw, through this picturesque screenshot of Sissy and Emily, that that's exactly what I was doing.

When the Champagne was empty, Emily asked if she should open another. Had we been alone, I would have opposed it, but Sissy was clearly in the mood, so I didn't object, though I didn't drink much more.

Eleanor never would have drank with us, at least not excessively. She hadn't been as strict as my family, but she disapproved of drunkenness, at least in front of other people.

Privately, the two of us had drunk enough wine to weaken our livers, and she'd gone through tee-totaling phases followed by weeks of unrestrained indulgence.

When the next bottle was empty, Sissy and I went to bed.

In slurred words, she asked me to take her photo, but I refused. She cocked her head coquettishly, asking if I'd rather undress her, which I wanted to do, but I didn't want to devour her as she had the Champagne.

"I want to get away," I admitted.

"What?" she drew her head back from our embrace.

"Just for the weekend."

"With Emily?"

"No. With you"

"Why?"

"Why not?"

She interlaced her fingers behind my neck, tugging my face close as she countered with a coy smile, "Why not?"

CHAPTER THIRTEEN

E xcept for the cities, the long stretches of the interstate were meditatively reassuring with their markings of familiar towns that, when I had left Texas, had been but blips on the map, old ghost towns that, over the past seven years, had been repainted to look like living saloons and tourist traps.

The improvement of rest stops was a welcome change to the once seedy gas stations the state was sadly known for. Yet somehow, I missed the grungy, outdated Western aura from my girlhood.

About three-quarters of the way through the trip, I pulled off at a gas station and shook Sissy, asking if she needed to use the bathroom. She'd fallen asleep as soon as we'd rolled out of the driveway.

Tiredly, she shook her head and rolled back over. I readjusted her blanket before filling up the car. When I went into the store, I bought her some candy and myself a coffee, and as I was paying, I paused to glance up at the TV behind the cashier.

As one of those millions of Americans who never bothered to vote, I hadn't even thought about the election.

The cashier glanced back to the TV when he realized I hadn't heard him tell me the total.

The store was empty, and he didn't seem to mind the delay.

Leaning onto the counter, he made a comment about how close the election was. He'd never thought Texas would come this close to blue.

My eyes bounced back to him, and I made an effort to shine a smile through my mask. "The elections get crazier every year," I answered.

He laughed, his head bobbing up and down. I pulled out my wallet and stuck my credit card in the machine. As it beeped, he slid a small bowl under the plastic shield that had been erected because of the pandemic.

"Happy Halloween," he said, and as I reached my hand in, I wondered what diseases I had caught Halloweens past by sticking my hand in the same bowl as hundreds of other kids.

I pulled out the credit card and picked up two Jolly Ranchers. "One for my girlfriend," I explained as he raised an eyebrow when I took a second.

He nodded, but with the mask, I couldn't tell if his expression was one of approval or judgment.

"Have a nice day," I said.

He echoed my sentiments, turning back to the television with a bored expression. A commercial for Lana Lane's newest movie started playing. As I rushed to get back to the car, I pushed memories of making love to Lana from my mind as I unwrapped the bundle of fruity sugar, my heart tingling at the small, insignificant interaction I'd had with the cashier.

He was the first stranger I'd spoken to in months.

Though when I had first met Sissy months ago, she had been a stranger, and now we were close enough that I didn't mind that she slept the rest of the way until just before we crossed the bridge to Galveston Island.

After rubbing sleep from her eyes, she yawned and stretched out her joints as though she'd been frozen for weeks, letting the blanket slip to reveal skin that had darkened despite the bruises having faded.

Over the past few weeks, she'd been helping Emily with various tasks around the ranch when she wasn't in school, and her tan proved it.

She rolled down the window, closing her eyes as she rested her head against the back of the seat, letting gusts of salty air blow through her hair.

"Turn on some music if you want," I told her, nodding to my phone.

"What kind of music do you like?" she asked, reminding me there were so many basic things we didn't know about one another.

"I actually don't listen to music very often. It distracts me from my work," I admitted, but I went on to name a few artists I liked.

She nodded, scrolling through the phone. "So, folksy, singer-song-writer kind of vibe?"

"I suppose you could call it that."

"That doesn't fit our beach party vibe."

"I didn't know we were going for a beach party vibe."

"We're at the beach."

"Yeah, but I guess I was thinking more of a romantic, enchanted cottage by the sea kind of vibe."

"We're not in England."

"But we're not in Florida," I countered but told her to pick whatever she liked. She put on something I'd never heard before, but I was too focused on traffic to listen.

Then we reached the ocean, and I had to yell over the wind to ask her to roll the window up as I turned down the music to glance at the sea from the corner of my eye.

Eleanor and I had often come here in high school, eager to escape our parents with bonfires and drinks on the beach. We came in spring, which she found dull because it wasn't hurricane season. Whenever the wind picked up, she'd stand on a balcony with her arms outstretched. When the winds strengthened, I'd pull her inside, and we'd laugh it off with whiskey.

I turned onto the street where the rental condo was, and for a second, the ocean lay bare before us, stretching endlessly over the sand. I smiled as I caught Sissy grinning from the corner of my eyes.

Pulling the car into the driveway, I paused before shutting off the engine, letting the music take me back to late-night dance parties on the weekend, not unlike this one.

When I finally switched the engine off, I leaned forward, pulling Sissy in for a kiss, but almost as soon as our lips touched, I heard screaming.

"Mommy! Those two women are kissing!"

I jerked back, turning my head to glare at a little boy who couldn't have been more than seven and was pointing a finger at us. I craned my neck to find his family. Their minivan was covered in religious bumper stickers, and by the looks of it, they were staying in the condo next to ours.

I winked at Sissy as I pushed open the car door. "Well, this is going to be a fun weekend."

Sissy sunk into her seat, hiding her face from the boy whose parents were telling him not to look.

Externally, her bruises had faded, but internally, they would always hurt.

"He's just a kid. He doesn't know any better."

"I know," she nodded.

I leaned over to give a kiss of reassurance, but she shifted, eyeing the family that was almost out of sight.

"Go on in," I said. "I'll get our bags."

She went inside, and when I opened up the trunk, the father adjusted his oversized pants and cleared his throat as he approached, out-stretching a hand and offering a name so generic I forgot it instantly.

"Kitty," I answered, offering my hand.

"Well, Ms...?"

"Kunz," I answered as I withdrew my hand.

His bushy eyebrow lifted. "Have I seen you before somewhere?"

I shrugged, not wanting to accuse this man of having watched a leaked lesbian sex tape or bring Eleanor into the conversation.

"Well, Ms. Kunz, my wife and I have the kids here and we wouldn't want them to be exposed to any ... negative influences."

"Don't worry. We're not throwing a party."

"Good to hear, but that's not what I meant."

"What did you mean?"

He laughed nervously. "Look. It's a free country. I have no objection to you and your friend, but-"

"She's my girlfriend."

"Right. Well, if you wouldn't mind keeping your affection to yourselves, my wife and I would appreciate that."

"Oh, don't worry," I said as I slammed the trunk. We're not into threesomes—at least not with men. If your wife is interested, well, she knows where we're staying."

When I shut the door to the house, Sissy covered me with kisses, laughing as she looked over my shoulder at his sour face.

"I can't believe you said that!" she exclaimed.

I shrugged. "I've said worse."

"I'm beginning to think you are a negative influence."

"Get upstairs and I'll prove it," I teased, but we didn't make it farther than the kitchen table.

When the wine was gone and the waves settled into smooth, ceaseless rhythm, I asked Sissy if she would read to me.

"You've never asked me to read to you before."

"You don't have to if you don't want to."

"No, I will." She flicked on the lamp. The shade was old-fashioned, reflecting a shadow that trapped her silhouette in straight yet curved lines across the wall's uneven surface.

She kept the sheets tucked modestly over her breasts. Still, when she crawled back into bed, I rested my head against them, leaving a hand on her heart to feel the steady rise and fall of every beat and breath as she began.

The story was beautiful, but the plot did not distinguish itself from other works, and Sissy was at a stage in her art when her works were inevitable variations on the themes that haunted her.

The mother was absent. The father was abusive. The heroine was uncertain and needed a lover. The sex scenes alternated between ignorant and overly specific, shifting from fade to black to pornographic.

It was a long way from good, but she had a writer's way with words, a gift that couldn't be taught, only guided.

With this craft, I couldn't carry the torch of any character except one who cared, a partner devoted deeply to the actualization of a girl who, when she became a woman, would change the world with her words as she had my heart with syllables moving in and out while waves washed over sand and waned out to sea, my breaths beginning to slow, my heart beating steadily to sleep.

Dreaming, the fully waxed moon shed light on the lines of a young woman's figure, illuminating eyes too beautiful to be bright, skin so smooth it couldn't be soft, touch so tender it had to be true.

Making love to me in the way I desired to be loved, she touched me with whispers and kisses I was ashamed to want, withdrawing a me only she could see until, waking, waves crashed against the rocks and cries carried from the balcony.

I rose from the bed, rubbing sleepy crusts from the sides of my eyes as I knelt beside her. I took her hands in mine, rubbing them for warmth against the wind. I left my head on her lap and wrapped my arms around her waist.

"What's wrong?"

Her answer was a hush. "You bit me."

"What?" I asked.

"I thought you had to be awake. We were having sex. And it was good. Better than it's ever been. It was like you knew everything I didn't even know I wanted."

She was too shy to give specifics, but if I'd done what Eleanor had done to me in the dream, she didn't need to.

"Then, when I was coming, you ..."

Tears cut off her words.

She said it, and I shook my head, apologizing, but she kept on.

"And I was crying for you to stop, and then I realized you weren't even awake for any of it."

"Did I hurt you?"

Her look answered for her.

"Sissy, I'm sorry. I would never do that."

"But you did."

"I didn't know!"

"Did you do that with Lana Lane?"

"No."

"With her?"

"With isn't the right word."

"Then what is the proper preposition for biting vaginas?"

"She liked pain."

"Do you like pain?"

"No!" I insisted as I wiped aside tears and looked out to the ocean, imagining the seafoam rising to Eleanor's ankles. She smiled, flashing teeth as sharp as a shark's.

I shivered.

Waves rolled over the sand, and as they rushed back to sea, the voice of the boy staying next door stretched across the sand. His father's hatred resounded in my head, and suddenly, I yearned to take Sissy's hand and promise it would be alright, but, when I thought of Eleanor, I wasn't sure what promises I could make.

"I don't want more pain," she said.

"Hurting you is the last thing I want to do."

"I know."

She stroked my hair, easing the truth out of me in my tiredness and guilt.

"She was cruel. Jealous, angry. She didn't know when to stop. Whenever I said I didn't want something, she only did it harder, as though she wanted to prove I should like it."

"Does Emily know?"

"No. I've never told anyone. Not even Lana. Especially not Emily."

"Then tell me. Everything."

So I spilled my soul, sparing no undesirable detail and confessing my uncertainty over the moment I'd ceased being a virgin, which at times I'd felt we'd never been since we'd begun before we knew what we were doing, only doing what felt right even though none of it had been, but none of it had been wrong.

"Is what we're doing wrong?" I asked as I came to the end.

"According to our neighbors, yes."

My laughter broke my tears.

"I didn't feel right until I found you," she admitted.

I took her in my arms, kissing her to confess the same.

We nestled into the embrace, closing our eyes and listening to the waves.

"This isn't what I expected from this weekend," she laughed.

My laughs echoed hers as I teased, "And it's only just begun."

CHAPTER FOURTEEN

S issy held me that night, though she was wary of sex, and the following day I was glad my dreams had been blank.

I kissed her cheek, but she didn't stir.

Her breaths were soft, the rise and fall of her chest heavy.

My camera was close, and the suggestion of its proximity made me imagine the image a lens could capture.

The sheets hid her body while revealing her curves, and when the breeze brushed through the windows, the fabric rustled like the surface of the sea.

Such an image deserved detail a sketch couldn't provide, but if it was so good, it didn't deserve the digitalization of my DSLR.

My memory would fade, and with it, the affection and attention for the minute, but with a picture, this moment would cease being mine and mine alone.

I kissed Sissy's cheek again, but still, she did not stir.

Letting my nose linger by her hair, I smelled the shampoo she still used even though there were better brands in our shower, savoring the sensation of salt mingling with her scent before I decided to start the day and make coffee before sitting on the porch with the book I'd been meaning to finish for ages, one of Sissy's favorites, a classic I should have read already, reading farther than I anticipated in a single sitting when Sissy pulled me back to reality.

"Sorry! I didn't mean to scare you!" she laughed as she drew her lips away from my cheeks once my shoulders had settled from their jump.

"I didn't hear you come down. Is there still coffee?" I asked as I realized my cup was empty.

"The pot's almost full. I think you made it too strong. I can smell it from here."

I sniffed but smelled only salt. "How would you know? You don't even drink coffee," I said over my shoulder as I went to the kitchen, though as I poured the next cup, I agreed I'd overloaded the filter in hopes of replicating the strength of Emily's espresso machine.

When I came outside, she was staring at the sea.

The beach itself was not beautiful. The water was not crystal clear, the sand color indistinct. Compared with the standard computer background, it failed to impress. Still, the ocean itself, with its ceaseless horizons and endless motion, would never cease to stir my soul.

"What should we do today?" Sissy asked, reminding me our time here was limited.

After yesterday, I didn't dare joke about having sex all day.

We went back and forth with a few ideas, ultimately deciding on a stereotypical long walk along the beach.

When we set out for our sandy stroll, the family from next door averted their eyes, but that was the extent of their unwanted attention.

We refrained from bringing our cameras so we could live in the moment, yet even without a brush or an aperture, my mind was constantly on my canvas, a subject to which we inevitably came.

"You told me once it didn't matter if one wanted to be an artist or not," Sissy said, "One simply is or isn't one."

"Yes, but being a professional artist is another matter," I countered.

"Did you always want to be one?"

"I was lucky. I didn't have to decide. I was granted the first fellowship I applied for and had a good opening show."

"Do you think I have what it takes?" she asked, her fingers tightening around mine.

"Yes," I answered.

The conversation shifted, returning to an insignificant matter and, as we spotted a political sign, the election.

At Rosewood, it was easy to forget that there was a world beyond the ranch. Meanwhile, for nearly everyone outside, it must have seemed society was collapsing.

A pandemic still raged, the economy suffered, and the fate of our country teetered like a see-saw.

"Have you really not told your family you're here?" she asked when we reached the point at which we'd agreed to turn back for the house.

"Would you tell your father?"

"Good point," she said, tucking a strand of hair behind her ear. "But it's just my father and me. You have brothers and sisters. And a mother."

"I don't want to see them, and I don't think they want to see me."

"And the friends you went to dinner with the night we met at the gas station?"

"The dinner was a disaster. I should have known it would be bad, but I suppose I wanted some connection to my past aside from Emily. And I saw you, so it wasn't a wasted evening."

I squeezed her hand as she blushed, and her eyes dropped to the sand.

"Oh look! A sand dollar!" She leaned down and picked it up, brushing off the sand. "I've been wanting to ask you about something," Sissy admitted.

We stopped, and my heart swirled at the sight of her eyes sparkling as they beheld the thin shell nestled in her palm.

"I've heard rumors. About a scene you made at Eleanor's funeral."

"I was wondering when you were going to ask, though I thought you'd ask about the sex tape first."

"No. I understand why you did that. Who wouldn't make a sex tape with Lana Lane?"

"I looked out to the calm sea, wishing the waves were louder so they could cover the sound of my voice. "It's true what I said at the funeral—at least most of it is. It depends on what you've heard. But I did say what I said—four words, five syllables."

She said them for me.

"Eleanor died a virgin."

I nodded.

I'd been asked to give a speech, and those were the only words I'd said. Then, I'd stepped away from the altar and left the church in silence.

"But it's not true," she protested.

"She never had a penis inside her."

"That's not the definition of a virgin."

"For some people it is."

"Was it for her?"

I dropped my hand from Sissy's, stuffing my hands in my back pockets.

"Eleanor was obsessed with the idea of virginity. She was fanatical about it. She swore she would never let a man touch her, and she refused even to talk about the subject. And you know Emily. You wouldn't believe they were mother and daughter the way they each talked about sex. It drove Eleanor mad. And whenever I so much as looked at a man, or another woman, she lost it. She threatened to kill herself other times."

"In the same way?"

"No. That's the sort of thing you can only pull off once."

She'd killed herself with a method so mad it made international news. I'd been in London and was forced to suffer seeing her face splattered over the TV with annoying accents. There was no image of her body, so they'd used an innocent photo from several years before. It wasn't a photo I'd taken.

"Is it true that Emily shot the bull? Even once it was dead?"

"Wouldn't you?"

"I don't know."

A wave rushed to my toes, and we altered our path to avoid the incoming tide.

"Did you really attend Eleanor's funeral with Lana Lane?"

"Lana felt guilty about what happened." The suicide was only weeks after the sex tape had been leaked. "And she wanted to support me. But she didn't sit by me. That wouldn't have been appropriate."

"Were the two of you together when Eleanor died?"

"I'm not sure what we were," I admitted, "I'm not sure what I was with Eleanor, either."

The water was becoming louder by the second as the volume of the rushing wind increased. Sissy gripped my hand, and I pulled her close as though to prevent the breeze from blowing her away, even though we knew the wind would not become so strong.

An echo of Eleanor's laughter rose over the wind, but I pressed on and held Sissy close.

When we reached the house, the door slammed with a gust.

"What are we?" she asked, nearly out of breath.

"What do you want us to be?" I hung my coat, releasing my hair from its ponytail and combing out the sea-blown tangles with my fingers.

"I don't want to be one of your flings," she continued.

"Who told you I had flings?"

"Emily."

"What else did Emily tell you?"

"A lot."

I laughed, but then I nodded. It was right of her to warn Sissy.

"She said your heart is broken."

I took Sissy in my arms and ran my fingers across the edges of her wind-brushed hair. "Whenever I look into people's eyes, I see Eleanor. But not in yours."

"There's something more I want to do," Sissy managed between breaths.

"What?"

"Turn the camera on you."

CHAPTER FIFTEEN

Seeing the same stretches of highway in reverse reminded me that between Rosewood and the ocean, there was civilization and Texas was not as removed from the rest of the world as the rest of the world liked to think.

There were political signs and not all for one party.

Remnants of Halloween remained, and I succumbed to capitalism's temptations by buying cheap candy.

Sissy fell asleep again, and I used the meditative silence to contemplate the undeveloped photos she'd taken and the sex that had followed.

For the first time, she'd taken control.

Whether it was the soothing of the waves or the clicking of a shutter that encouraged me to agree, the result had been more pleasurable than I'd anticipated. I felt its freeing effects in the smallest of ways, from the indulgences in mass-marketed chocolate to my disregard of the speed limit until Sissy stirred and made a gagging sound.

"I think I'm gonna be sick."

I asked if I should pull over, and she moaned yes.

The car hadn't been stopped for a second when she threw open the door and vomited.

I switched off the engine and scrambled for water.

"Do you want to lie down in the back seat?" I asked. Her face was pale, her eyes droopy. We'd had wine the night before, but not enough to make her so sick.

She shook her head, saying it was car sickness, and she'd just lean the seat back. As soon as I started driving, she was out again.

For the rest of the trip, I continued eating candy and musing over quasi-philosophical thoughts, pondering the nature of love and wondering why Sissy stirred my soul as no other woman had.

Despite the excess of time, I found no answers.

As we approached Rosewood, I was robbed of the opportunity to admire its grandeur by Sissy's second round of sickness.

Before the car fully stopped, she'd opened the door to throw up, and Emily, tearing gardening gloves from her skin, rushed to her side.

Given there was a pandemic, I admired Emily's disregard for disease. Considering her overwhelming maternal instinct, I doubt it even occurred to her that she might catch a virus by embracing Sissy.

"Oh, darling, let's get you upstairs," she said as she felt the girl's forehead.

Within a quarter of an hour, Sissy had been tucked into bed, had her temperature taken, and been given something to settle her stomach and help her sleep.

"If it were carsickness, it would've settled quickly," Emily explained as she came downstairs, "but she's not coughing, so I doubt it's Covid. How do you feel?"

"Fine. But if she has something, I'll catch it soon."

"We both will. You look good, though. Good sex?"

I rolled my eyes. "Not everything in a relationship revolves around sex."

"No, but most of it does. Trust me, I was married twenty-three years."

"And divorced."

"Exactly why you should listen. Coffee?"

"Always, but I think I'll jog first. I've been sitting for too long."

After changing clothes and checking on Sissy, I ran my usual route, observing the alterations of autumn.

The leaves hadn't shifted colors and had at the same time instead of piling gradually. The ground was dry, so the leaves ripped under the weight of my strides.

My speed was good. It usually was when my mind was spinning.

I was worried about Sissy and concerned I might get sick, but more than that, I thought of the portrait.

I couldn't paint Eleanor in her prime, nor could I ignore the aspects of her that haunted me.

As I ran past the barn, I sped up, not yet able to face the darkest image of all.

Out of breath when I returned, I showered quickly and checked on Sissy.

She was still asleep.

I accepted the coffee, but when Emily spoke, her words went through my ears.

"Are you alright?" she asked.

Her gaze was soft, so gentle I couldn't bear to burden it with my troubles.

When she saw the painting, she would be forced to face the darker side of Eleanor.

Until then, I would spare her innocence, especially when Sissy needed her.

But ignorance was a luxury I could not afford.

"Yeah," I answered as I placed my mug in the dishwasher. "I just need to paint."

CHAPTER SIXTEEN

O n an early summer's eve seven years hence, when the wind was so still that only bugs were to be heard, a young woman in a simple summer dress and worn leather boots approached the barn.

With its chipping red paint and bleachy white windows, it was quintessentially quaint, but the barns are hollow. Within its wooden frames awaited a beast pent-up with energy from confinement, readying itself for the rodeo when the bravest of cowboys would dare to mount it. Their hopes were only for eight seconds.

Eleanor's ambitions were far greater.

Striding as though she didn't hear the bull's snarling or see its horns twisting from a head twice the size of her own, she ignored the clangs of its heavy weight as it thrust itself from side to side, denting the cage's iron bars.

As she climbed the side of the gate, she realized she'd brought a rope but no glove, but it didn't matter. The end would be the same.

Still, she wanted to do things right, so she struggled to tie the rope around a horn, scraping the skin of her wrist as she managed a loose loop.

She would have smiled as she swung her legs over the animal and felt it jerk under her body. She might have said a prayer but probably cursed, and I suspect she was afraid the moment she kicked open the gate.

And in this second, the portrait was born.

After the moment it captured, she would last the whole eight seconds, no matter what it took, and when the beast threw her, she didn't run but faced it head-on.

Her skull cracked, spilling brains over dirt to be ignored by the animal as it rampaged over her bruising, breathless body until someone heard the noise.

Her father shot the beast.

Once it was dead, her mother seized the shotgun and mutilated it until there was less of it than there was of Eleanor.

The body was removed before they could really see, so I came to identify it.

But that was excess information.

Art was a condensation of character, extrapolation of sensation. And there was no moment more significant in Eleanor's life than when she mounted that bull and decided to die. To paint any other moment would be false, but to face this moment was agony.

To hold a brush is already torture. To stare at a blank canvas is even greater torture. To hold a brush to a blank canvas to paint Eleanor's suicide was to pierce open my flesh and bleed acrylic.

Every stroke, each alteration seared stains from my soul onto what, in the end, was nothing more than a piece of cloth, a shroud etched with Eleanor's outline.

I don't know how much I had painted when I stopped. It could have only been a base layer or background scenery. Most likely, it was not much at all, but it was a beginning.

"You didn't wash behind your ears," Emily muttered as she took a rag and switched on the sink. I squirmed as the wet fabric touched my freshly dried skin. She laughed, squeezing my earlobe and wiggling it while showing me the paint smears on the rag as though I were a toddler returning from art class. Picking up another, Emily wiped away the dampness and declared, "All clean."

"At least for now," I muttered as I moved to fix my coffee.

At some point, I'd fallen asleep on the couch in my studio. The stiffness of my muscles urged me never to do it again, though I doubted my mind would listen.

"Did you sleep well?" I asked, glancing over my shoulder and spotting her newspaper, unwrapped but unopened. My eyes flickered to the clock, and then, from the corner of my eyes, I spotted something else upon which Emily's eyes were fixed.

When I turned back around, she still hadn't answered.

I approached to see what it was.

A single beat slammed inside my chest, and suddenly my heart stilled.

The cup and saucer wobbled under my grip. Emily set them on the counter for me as she drew my face close to hers again, this time for a kiss atop my head. I withdrew as soon as her lips pulled back, shaking my head as I clenched my cup and drained as much caffeine as I could.

I wasn't ignorant enough to believe it belonged to Emily, but my disbelief demanded I ask.

She scoffed without cynicism. "I'm flattered you think I'm so young. And who would you suppose the father is?"

"I don't know who you sleep with. More coffee?"

She slid her cup to me. "I suppose so since Sissy's not having any."

I felt my face scowl as I steamed the milk. "She doesn't even drink coffee."

"True. The only thing she'll have to give up is alcohol."

"And her youth."

After visiting Sissy's home, I offered Emily a summary of what I knew about Sissy's encounter with her ex-boyfriend. The details had remained a secret even from me, so I'd hoped he hadn't coerced or forced her into sex, though the cries in her sleep and hesitation in bed had caused me to suspect the truth.

"She doesn't know yet."

I shivered as I wiped the froth from the milk steamer. "You mean she took the test and didn't want to know the answer?"

"No, I had her pee into a plastic cup. Told her it was a new type of Covid test."

If my mind weren't numb, I might have laughed.

"What should we tell her?"

"The truth. If we don't tell her, she'll figure out eventually."

I flipped the switch for espresso, watching and waiting for the dark liquid to drop until the drips became creamy so I could flip the switch and pour the milk, wishing that the only arts to master in life were eating, sleeping, and breathing.

To settle my tremors as I slid her the saucer, Emily rested her hand over mine.

"I'll tell her," she promised, and when I tried to object, she squeezed my hand. "She's had a lover all weekend. Now she needs a mother."

Relentingly, I removed my hand from her hold. I intersected my fingers around the cup, which, despite the heat, felt cold compared with the tenderness of Emily's touch.

"She's not ready to be a mother," I said.

"No woman is ready to be a mother," she countered.

"You at least had a husband. And this house. And money."

"She has you. And me. And this house. And who else am I going to spend my money on?"

My fingers tightened around the handle. "You want her to keep it?"

Emily sighed, and I could tell from her heavy breath that the answer was yes but that she wouldn't say so.

She'd come to love Sissy as her own, but in a year, Sissy would be off to college, and who knew if she would return to Rosewood? A baby would force her to stay and bring another love into Emily's otherwise barren life.

"Were you working on the portrait all night?" she asked, and I stiffened at the change of subject. Seeing my discomfort, she added, "If you weren't, it's fine. There's no rush."

"No, I was," I nodded, unable to admit that it wasn't that which had disturbed me but the fact that the Eleanor I'd painted wasn't one I was ready for her to see.

Thankfully, she didn't press.

Strange, when I thought that just hours ago, I had been immersed in the last seconds of my lover's life, and now I was contemplating the first stages of a life my love might bear.

Had my sleep been more restful. I might have expressed more shock or reacted more strongly, but as it was, I could only sip my coffee.

Emily seemed in an equal state. She was always thoughtful, but she rarely shared her pensive side. To me, constancy of determination defined her, but I knew better than anyone that she only appeared so because of intensely private and secret strife.

Ordinarily, she hid this from me, but at this moment, I was grateful she didn't, so I knew I was not alone in my loss for words when Sissy froze at the foot of the stairs, her hands clutching the rail as her puffy eyes fixed on the unmistakably positive pregnancy test.

CHAPTER SEVENTEEN

S kin encasing other skin ceases to be its own, but when has skin ever been an isolated entity? I wondered as I stroked the external layers of the epidermis that now compelled and repulsed me with foreign fascination.

This was the skin Sissy wore when she was in bed beside me, sexual yet only sleepily so, distinct from the skin she wore with Emily when they sat sensually on the couch, Sissy's head in Emily's lap and Emily stroking Sissy's hair as they spoke of subjects inconsequent, separate from the skin no one spoke of inside Sissy's, just as no one spoke of Eleanor's decaying skin, from which birthed the rotting flesh of my canvas as studio hours flickered by in dim lighting and damp air.

Emily insisted that windows needed to be opened as she came in daily to check that I breathed, thrusting open curtains and glowering wordlessly at the scenes smeared across the canvas.

She'd seldom entered this space before, and a week prior, my muscles might have tensed at her intrusion. Now they were numb even with the massaging of her fingers over my forehead.

"Sissy needs you," she said, but the fibers of my eardrum stood still despite the disruption of sound.

I swiveled in my stool as I answered that I would support whatever decision she made, my words distant, and as I spoke, my attention was on the colors in the composition. Without a second layer, they would fade.

"Do you think she can decide without your support?"

"You're blocking my light."

"Sometimes you're more impossible than my daughter was."

The complaint passed through my ears, and Emily left.

Thus, days passed, and days became weeks—two, perhaps three, to be as precise as possible.

It was selfish, wrong, cruel, and I knew it, but it was all I could do.

To explain how I closed my heart would take lifetimes of therapy, and even so, the immorality could not be ignored.

Sissy and I moved past it, and as there was no argument at the time, I shall spare the one that came later.

This stage of mourning – no other name suits – ended the second Sissy said she made her decision. She didn't want to keep the baby.

She didn't mention manipulation or rape, nor did she need to.

Emily disapproved, but she never said so and put on a solid face. It was what I'd wanted from the beginning, but I wouldn't admit it and put on a sad face.

When she asked if I'd go with her, I said of course.

The morning of the appointment, I woke without Sissy still curled up under the sheets next to me, so I could not kiss her as I usually did before stretching out like a cat and leaving her behind to sleep as long as she liked.

Her sleep had been restless lately. Mine had been sound.

Except for our interwoven hands, we slept to separate, sexless rhythms.

At breakfast, Emily went to the trouble of making Sissy hot chocolate, which I found childish despite sneaking a splash into my espresso before steaming my milk.

Emily hugged Sissy before we left.

There were no words between Emily and me—there hardly were these days except for her accusations about the stuffiness of my studio. Still, she sent me off with a kiss.

Despite having insisted on my company, Sissy didn't seem glad for it as she slumped into the passenger seat, an elbow propped up on the armrest with her head resting on her fist.

"My phone's in my purse if you want to put on some music," I suggested.

She shook her head.

"Do you want to talk?"

Another shake.

I settled into the silence, embracing the entrancement of driving as my consciousness transfigured into a series of exits and lane changes.

The clinic was on the outskirts of San Antonio. I was struck, as I had been during our drive to the beach, by how spaces had exploded into urban hamlets, making me mourn a West that, even in childhood, had not been entirely wild.

"If you're not sure, we don't have to do this today," I reassured her as we neared the clinic.

Her elbow was still stiffly propped on the side of the door, her head still settled on a clenched fist.

"I'm sure."

I swore as I turned into the parking lot.

At the end, opposite the clinic, stood a group of praying protestors.

They were silent, but their judging quietude resounded louder than aggressive shouts.

"Don't these people have anything better to do?" I complained as I rotated the keys, their silence strengthening as the parking lot became bereft of engine humming.

Sissy grabbed her bag without a word, avoiding eye contact with them as we went to the door, staying huddled under my arm until we made it.

Due to the pandemic, friends and family weren't allowed inside. From the looks of it, most of the other friends and family had opted to wait in their cars to avoid the looming protestor glares.

"I'll wait here by the door," I promised. "Unless you want me to go get you anything. Milkshake? Iced tea? Ice cream?"

"I'm fine."

After she put her mask on, but before she opened the door, I took her in my arms, kissing her first on her forehead and then over the cloth covering her face.

"I love you," I whispered, and at least she responded, albeit with a muffled mask voice.

The little window in the door was tinted, so I couldn't see anything beyond the first few steps she took, but I kept my eyes glued to the pane until the misery of waiting set on.

I'd brought a book, but as soon as I opened it, fantasy seemed frivolous, so I pulled out my phone, which seemed even more nonsensical. Even reading the news of the unresolved election seemed silly when I thought of what went on behind the other side of the wall.

I pulled my sunglasses over my eyes, keeping my phone in my hand as a method of avoiding eye contact with the protestors' glares.

There were about fifteen of them, mostly middle-aged women who dressed as though revealing anything beyond their ankles was scandalous. As I scanned the faces, I came across two that I would have been happy to never see again.

My stomach churned, and I considered breaking my promise to Sissy and hide in the car.

Buried in their Bibles, they hadn't recognized me.

Propping my head on my hand, I tried to discern the differences that age had put upon them, too distracted by Sissy to feel resentment.

For a few years, we'd still called on Christmas and birthdays, and at the beginning of the pandemic, there had been a text to make sure I wasn't rotting in a mass grave.

From the distance, it was evident that their fashions had not changed and that they had both put on weight.

When I saw the stroller and realized it belonged with them, my heart bounced, and I had to cover my mouth to keep from releasing a sound.

I'd known there was going to be a baby, but time had become so warped I had forgotten it must have already come. I scanned my brain for the timeframe, trying to recall if I'd seen any cards or announcements. If I remembered right, the baby must have come in August, after I'd already moved back to Texas.

I stood, coiling my fingers around the railing as I fought the urge to go to them. It felt wrong to associate with them when Sissy was inside, but the decision was made for me.

"Katherine?"

I rushed down the steps, letting my heart do all the leaping it wanted as I let myself be embraced. It had been years since anyone had called me that, and despite myself, I was smiling.

Then, pulling back from our hug, my sister looked over my shoulder at the clinic. "Are you-"

"No!" I shook my head violently, debating how to explain and deciding quickly on offering as little information as necessary. "I'm waiting for someone."

Tucking a strand of hair behind my ear, I turned, giving a dutiful nod to the woman beside her, but it wasn't fear of viruses that kept me from leaping into my mother's arms.

"Mom," I muttered politely, sucking in air as my eyes fell to the ground.

I don't know if it was her added weight or age, but her power to hover over me had only magnified.

She came forward and hugged me as though it were an obligation, tapping my back lightly. She looked me up and down. I awkwardly pulled my sunglasses back over my head, letting her see that my blue eyes hadn't changed.

"I'm sorry I haven't called. I've been busy," I explained with an excuse that, though always true, was not a lie, eagerly awaiting a nod of understanding or acknowledgment of innocence. My mother merely let her hands drop from my sides, silently lost in her own thoughts until my sister intervened.

"This is Andy. Do you want to hold him?"

My heart leaped with my grin as my attention shifted to the stroller.

"Can I hold him? If you don't want me to because of Corona, I understand."

Behind me, my mother's scoff made her disbelief in the virus clear.

"Oh, I don't care about that," my sister laughed.

My heart melted as I tucked my fingers under the little baby's arms, bringing him close to my chest as I searched for features like my own, but he took after his father more than my sister.

"Aren't you precious?" I asked even though I knew Andy couldn't answer, but based on his gurgles, he could at least understand my affection. I brought his face close to my own, kissing his round button nose and hovering my lips over the top of his head as I swayed from side to side, savoring his baby scents.

"This is your Aunt Kitty," my sister told him as she tickled his back. "She's a famous artist."

I laughed and gave a little eye roll as I switched my arms around, tugging him closer. "Famous is a bit of an exaggeration." Infamous might have been appropriate, considering my name was intertwined with Lana Lane's sex tape and Eleanor's suicide.

My mother asked how Mrs. Pontell was.

"She's doing well," I answered instinctively. "She's asked me to do a portrait. It's why I'm here. Well not here, but here."

"And why are you here?"

The door to the clinic flung open before I could answer, and Sissy stood at the steps, her head jerking from side to side as she tore the cloth mask from her face. When she saw me, she rushed to me. I hurried to hand the baby to my sister, stumbling back as Sissy's body flung itself into mine, her arms squeezing my frame as tears flowed over my shoulders. I wrapped my arms around her, cuddling her head in my hands as she shook.

"Shsh, it's alright," I whispered, looking over her shoulder at my mother and sister, whose jaws had dropped in confusion.

I closed my eyes, shutting out their stares as I pressed a kiss into her forehead.

"I can't do it," she said between sobs, and as I opened my eyes, I could see satisfaction on my mother's face.

"That's alright," I reassured her with another kiss.

She tugged her head back, looking up into my eyes.

I whimpered at their redness, wiping tears from her cheeks.

"Will you take me home?"

I nodded, kissing her forehead, and for the first time, I resisted her kiss as she pressed her lips against mine. My eyes closed for a second, only to shoot open as I heard my mother's repulsive gasp. I should have kissed her even more fiercely after that, but I pulled away, shifting my eyes sideways as I took Sissy by the hand, turning away from them towards the car.

As I led her across the parking lot, Sissy glanced over her shoulder, suppressing her tears enough to ask, "Do you know those people?"

I opened the door for her, and as soon as she crawled into the seat, I checked around the side of the car to see if they were watching.

They were gawking.

While she pulled the buckle over her chest, I caught Sissy by surprise with a forceful, passionate kiss, cupping her cheeks in my hand.

"Yes," I admitted, but I barely had time to breathe between that and the kiss that she gave me back.

CHAPTER EIGHTEEN

A shamed of my shame in front of my family and too ashamed to admit to Sissy they were my family, I compensated by sharing sweet sex I'd learned from women whose names I'd forgotten or never learned. When Sissy offered to return my favors, I whispered she should sleep, with which she seemed content, and once she was snoring, I snuck out to my studio and dozed off with a brush in hand.

The ashes of Eleanor's skin had risen, and from them burned a passionate piece of near abstraction, every stroke a flame of her heart or a flicker of her wit, the colors so intense anyone save me would not have recognized them and their shapes as Eleanor's bones and blood as I passed the days playing with her forms.

At dinner, my mind lingered beside them, my body existing between Emily and Sissy's conversations that seldom addressed the life budding inside Sissy's body.

Sissy's mind wasn't settled, and so long as it didn't need to be, neither Emily nor I would pressure her.

One morning, after a long night of painting, I woke to blinding sunshine sneaking through the curtains. The paint had dried under my fingernails. Splotches stuck to my skin.

I made a half-hearted effort to tidy up before going downstairs for coffee, which fueled the continuation of the painting.

My shoulders jumped when I entered the kitchen.

A young, tanned cowboy was sipping the last of a café americano as he covered his disheveled hair with a hat.

"Miss Kunz," he nodded politely as he placed the cup in the dish-washer.

I barely managed a good morning as he brushed past, leaving traces of Emily's perfume.

Emily emerged from her room with her hair less carefully brushed than usual and her smile more secretive.

"You're up early," she said as she took his place by the espresso machine.

"Has he been here all night?" I asked, trying to remember what had happened after dinner. I'd gone up to my studio after dessert without seeing Sissy or Emily again.

"No. He comes in early to milk the goats."

"We have goats?"

"I have goats. Haven't you noticed on your jogs? They're next to the barn."

"Have I been missing the fact that he's here the whole time?"

"You don't wake up very early, and he doesn't come every day."

She switched on the machine, silencing my questions with its gur-gling.

When she slid me my cappuccino, I wrapped my fingers around the mug, curious how many empty coffee cups I'd overlooked in the dishwasher.

"He has to be younger than I am," I noted.

Emily scoffed. "Says the woman sleeping with a teenager."

"That's different! I'm not ..."

"Old?" She offered.

"I didn't say that."

She glanced at my hands and narrowed her eyes at the sticking paint but didn't say anything as she pulled out the pans.

There were goats by the barn.

Years ago, there had been cows, but they'd been moved after what happened with Eleanor.

I'd known the cows were gone. The goats shouldn't have shocked me. They were just goats, and that cowboy was just a fuck.

I pulled the newspaper from its sleeve, glancing at the headlines. The election was supposedly determined, but debates about which candidate had won still dragged on.

Since returning with Sissy from the clinic and even before that, when we'd come home from the beach, the world marched on, sweeping up Emily and Sissy with it while I splattered myself with overpriced paint.

When I glanced up from the paper, Emily was staring with piqued eyebrows and an amused grin.

I never bothered looking at the paper anymore. I'd even stopped skimming the arts and culture section.

As I sipped my coffee, I looked back down at the words while Emily stopped staring and started cracking eggs.

I thought of the cowboy and the way the veins in his forearms had tightened as he gripped the rim of his hat, his mischievous, boyish smile, imagining him bragging with the boys about how he'd shoved his dick inside Mrs. Pontell.

The pages tensed between my fingers as I thought of Emily smothering him with kisses, holding him like a baby.

She adjusted the knob on the stove. Gas clicked. A fire hummed.

"I'm going to Louisiana over the weekend," she said as she spooned a chunk of grease into the pan. An image of another lover popped into my mind as I thought of her sprawled on the porch of an old Acadian home, humidity dripping from her hair as a faceless man cried out in Creole. As she spoke of home, her accent slipped. "Sissy's comin' with me."

I swallowed the frothy remains of my coffee. "Why?"

"She needs a change of scenery."

Since Emily hadn't offered to take me, I didn't ask from what or whom.

"And because I want her to see some options for the future."

"Your house is hours from any college."

The crackling of fat settled as she poured the eggs into the pan.

"My cousin's daughter and her husband have been trying to have a baby for years."

"I thought you would want to raise the baby here."

Emily laughed as she looked at me over her shoulder. "Darlin', I'm fifty-seven. I don't have the energy for that anymore."

"You have the energy to fuck a twenty-year-old."

She flicked off the stove.

My lips tightened as she dished me a generous serving.

"I'm sorry," I murmured.

"Eat your eggs before they get cold."

She didn't touch her own plate, and as she went to the espresso machine, I realized she had waited until I was fed to make her own coffee, which should have made my food taste better but only made my stomach spin with guilt.

Once her coffee was ready and she'd taken a few bites, she turned the newspaper around and glanced over the front page. She flipped a page before speaking.

"She needs to make up her mind before the end of the month. I don't want to make her decision for her, but she can't make one without choices, and you're not helping her."

"I'm supporting her!"

"Just like that young man is supporting me."

I shivered at the comparison.

"Sex is an important part of a relationship. Sometimes the most important part. But Thomas and I had great sex. And our relationship was screwed up. I don't want you to make my mistakes. Or my daughter's."

"What do you mean?" I asked.

She looked up from the paper, and I squirmed under her gaze's pity. Looking back down, she turned another page.

"I should have said more when you two were together. I won't make that mistake again."

At the other end of the table, I heard muesli crunching under Eleanor's teeth as she glared down at my fatty eggs, not needing to lecture me on cholesterol and praise the health benefits of her foreign-dried fruits since she'd done that years ago.

"I love Sissy."

"And my daughter loved you."

"What's that supposed to mean?"

"Sweetie, I know all those bruises didn't come from your father."

My jaw stiffened. "I would never hurt Sissy."

"She told me you did at the beach."

"I was asleep!"

"You've been asleep for weeks," she countered. "Do you know she's been accepted to five colleges already and that when you go into your studio every day she cries because she can't make up her mind and is too afraid to ask you for help? Do you have any idea how much it hurts me to watch you ignore her so you can go sleep with art supplies? You need to open your eyes, Kitty."

The eggs had gone cold. I could tell because they'd stopped steaming and were mushing into the plate. I'd hardly touched them. There were few tastes more unpleasant than cold eggs, especially eggs cooled by neglect.

"I thought painting this portrait would help you, but it was selfish of me. I won't let it destroy you."

I managed a bite of my cold eggs, cringing from my memory of my mother's admonitions about wasted food.

"While we're gone I think you should think about what you want. I'm never going to kick you out or tell you want to do, but I'm not going to let you hurt Sissy, and I don't want to see you hurt yourself. I care more about you than any painting."

She meant it kindly, and the warmth of her words tingled my heart.

But when they echo through my memory, all I can think about is how little Emily understood what it was to be an artist.

When she and Sissy left that weekend, I wandered through the empty rooms to marvel over memories.

In the kitchen, I painted watercolors, which I'd never liked but had been forced to create for a silly project. I'd sat with Eleanor at the counter with our plastic tubs of cheap paint and cups of dirty water when she accidentally knocked her juice over my paper.

I cried.

Emily comforted me, and when she told her daughter to apologize, Eleanor spilled juice over her own picture instead of saying sorry. In Emily's room - I shouldn't have gone in, but I did - I sketched the rosary and the photo behind her bed. Outside, I photographed architectural details: Rosewood's imposing entrance in black and white, the back patio in sepia, the barn in colors that would have been bright if the wood weren't chipped.

The living room lent itself to the pastels I set up on the back of the piano so I could stand staring at the empty space where we'd once secretly gazed into each other's eyes behind Emily's back while Emily played. My studio was a space for oil, but as far as I recalled, it was a room we'd rarely spent time in, so without any materials, I approached Eleanor's bedroom, tracing the sign with my chipped fingernail.

A ROOM OF ELEANOR'S OWN.

The letters are unevenly sized, the text is off-center, the spaces inside the vowels are smudged, and the closing period is smeared into the last letter.

(Kitty's cage)

Neatly printed in thick permanent marker.

The color had faded, and if pressed, the sheet would tear.

I passed it every day, never noticing that meant Sissy did, too. As I imagined her jealousy as she passed by, I ripped the sign from its duct-taped corners and crumpled it, leaving the torn tape as dust jumped with the swinging of the door.

The bed was made with cotton tucked so tightly under the mattress that it looked like stiff stone. In her bathroom, the bristles on a toothbrush had hardened next to a tub nearly squeezed empty, with edges curled over in tight swirls. A single strand of hair rested tangled around a comb that I held to my nose, my nostrils scratching as the dust rose through my sinuses.

I sprayed her perfume, not the brand-name ones but the boutique ones she'd worn every day, sniffing until I could no longer smell.

On her desk, the pages of the legal pad had thinned and felt flaky under the oils left by my fingerprints. From the top drawer I pulled out a plastic folder of photographs preserved in glossy paper.

About the room, appropriate pictures of us with school uniforms and summer camp smiles were scattered.

The images hidden in the desk were unsuitable for walls and, as a grown woman, no longer appropriate for me.

At thirty-two, I shouldn't have shivered at an eleven-year-old Eleanor staring bravely into a camera with barely-formed bare breasts or become sweaty as a girl's lips separated in orgasm, touched myself when a young woman whispered she loved me.

Her head cocked up from the pillow, an eyebrow rising with the edge of her mouth. Her polished nails traced the spaces between her ribs before her hand flattened and ran its way down her waist to the bones enclosing her hips.

She had to touch herself?

Half-tease, half-command.

Unsure whether it was a question or demand, I seized her so she could seize and submerge me in sex.

There was no questioning when Eleanor came. In my arms, she came constantly and so strongly her moaning and crying never seemed to stop save to strangle me in satisfaction.

Musk caught in my throat, but I couldn't stop to open a window.

Her nails dug harder into my skin, scratching my scalp as the roots of my hair were yanked and the sides of my ears masticated.

Her hands curled around my wrists, pressing them into sheets thick with decay and desire. Even when she released, I didn't dare fight her handcuffs of dust as she suffocated me with softness, tying me with her tongue, loving me with lips and lies, her taste buds turning acid as she swallowed my skin, poisoning my pussy as I panted, her teeth driving into my clit as I came.

Crying, I curled my fingers around the roots of her hair, thrusting and throwing her head to the carpet, turning my face to hide my tears as, bit by bit, her body dissolved into dust.

The skin she'd caressed shattered in sweat.

My clothes are torn to tatters.

The wind whistled over the dust as I forced open the windowsill.

The photographs blew over the bed.

Emily and Sissy returned, not asking why Eleanor's room was open chaos, and found me painting not Eleanor on the canvas, but myself.

CHAPTER NINETEEN

I n paint, I was as realistic as in Sissy's photographs, the black and
white tones of which I tried to replicate by etching eyes I knew to
be blue and hair I'd heard was golden.

The self-portrait progressed quickly despite the reduced time I
dedicated to it, delving instead into Thanksgiving preparations.

I'd taken Emily's words to heart and was attentive to Sissy in
ways other than sex. She opened up about her hesitations concerning
adoption and the confusion brought about by hormones, sickness, and
countless changes in her life. Unable to escape her religious upbringing, she was adamantly against abortion, and I refrained from influenc-
ing her decisions as best I could, supporting her by sharing the progress
of the self-portrait, which brightened her since her pictures served as
its prototype. Between chats about oils and acrylic, we discussed the
traditions we'd like to carry on.

Sissy claimed she'd never celebrated with much more than re-heat-
ed, pre-cooked store-bought turkey slices. After years abroad, I was
eager for an all-American food coma.

I didn't ask what Emily had done for Thanksgiving the past seven
years, but her excitement suggested that she wanted to make up for
missed cranberry sauce.

In the old days, Thanksgiving at Rosewood had been a grand affair
even though it often consisted only of Emily, Thomas, Eleanor, and me.
I'd always start that Thursday at my home before finding an excuse

to leave. At my home, there was only fighting on the day intended for thanks, whereas for the Pontells, holidays were the only occasions Emily and Thomas agreed not to argue.

As the day approached, Emily began clearing Eleanor's bedroom, throwing nearly everything away. When she came across the folder of nude photographs and dirty poetry, she handed it to me, my face flushing despite the neutrality of her grin. I shoved the folder in a file, unopened.

Since I started to wake earlier and in my own bed instead of the studio, I encountered Emily's cowboy fuck more than before. I realized there was more than one of these boys and that when her lawyer friend swung by to give advice about some issue vaguely related to tax laws, I noticed he left with his gelled hair disheveled and that Emily was humming as she did the dishes. Despite her smile and the touch of my shoulder after these encounters, I found myself tingling as I thought about how they could only fuck her, whereas Thomas had made love, how I could only paint a copy of Eleanor, whereas Eleanor had lived feeling guilty while cherishing the fact that between her daughter and me, Emily made no distinction as she fed me generous helpings of dinners she'd spent hours cooking.

The only Thanksgiving task I was permitted to perform was grocery shopping.

Amongst the aisles where I'd first smelled Sissy, I came across Caroline.

She politely tried to strike up a conversation about something other than the disastrous dinner at her house. To be polite in return, I made an excuse about having to get home quickly.

"I've heard rumors, Kitty," she said sharply as I tried to make my escape.

"Rosewood attracts them," I replied.

"Your girlfriend's attracted to them. She's the only one at the high school still doing things online. I've heard she's pregnant."

Sissy had visited a doctor in town, and word traveled fast.

"I know you've been fed a lot of misinformation about lesbians, but we can't get each other pregnant." I walked away without saying more, glad that under my face mask, I was less recognizable, but even then, I felt eyes on me. As I reached the refrigerators in the back, I sensed the presence of a gaze I felt even when it wasn't there.

Her eyes squinted under the brightness of the white superstore lights, hardening as she froze with sticks of butter between her hands and the shopping cart, her expression impossible to read underneath the thin medical mask. Suspecting my mother's face was no kinder than when I'd seen her at the abortion clinic, I tossed an entire turkey into my basket and swung the cart around to head for the check-out.

Lana Lane was on the cover of a fashion magazine next to the candy bars. I thought about buying it just to make the onlookers talk, but I didn't want to make Sissy jealous.

That night was Wednesday, and in anticipation of a day of gratitude, I went down on Sissy for the first time since we'd gone to the beach, holding her hands until and while she came, keeping her close afterward, stroking her hair as her chest rose and fell to the rhythm of dreams as I dreamt with open eyes of adding color to my painting.

We both slept in and when her morning sickness woke us, I tied back her curls before brightening her face with dabs of moisturizer.

It was nearly noon when we went downstairs to discover a feast nearly complete and a bottle of wine half-finished.

Since the parade wasn't on, Emily had a romantic comedy running in the background. Over the female protagonist's dumb comments, Eleanor's nagging echoed around through the room. I doubt Emily heard since the first thing she did when we came down was ask, "Kitty, why is there an extra turkey? I told you I ordered a wild one."

I made an excuse about reading the list wrong. She didn't appear to believe it, but based on my distant tone, she knew better than to press.

"Well, you better both be hungry."

"Where is the turkey I bought?" I asked as I opened the fridge, glancing frantically at the oven to make sure she hadn't cooked two.

"The freezer downstairs."

Emily poured herself another glass of wine, and as I fired up the espresso machine, she and Sissy started chatting about the food. As the aromas of freshly ground beans and roasting poultry overwhelmed my olfactory glands, I thought back to the instant coffee in my parents' home and the clinking of iced tea glasses as my mother and sisters chattered about new recipes or holiday decorations. Enjoying the rare solitude that a holiday offered in our shared bedroom, a littler version of me colored or painted, counting the minutes until enough time would have passed for me to appropriately escape to Rosewood, asking either to be dropped off during a grocery run or, once I was old enough, borrow the car.

The clucking of chickens outside brought me back to the only year I hadn't been allowed to go because I was in trouble for swearing at Sunday school.

By then, I was old enough that Sunday school seemed childish, and I wouldn't have gone if I weren't forced to. No one in our family was forced to attend church, only threatened with shouts of damnation, a fact I used to try and defend my use of the phrase "go to hell," which earned me an extra week of grounding.

As I was doodling, my younger sister came in, grabbing my notebook.

"Whatcha drawin'?"

I rushed to hide the magazines I was working from, but it was too late. One of my brothers had also come.

"Look, Kitty has magazines of naked girls!" the little sister teased. My brother seized them, joining her laughter as they took to the stairs, shouting about their discovery at the top of their lungs.

I sprinted after them, but by the time we reached the family room, the magazines were in my father's hands.

One of my brothers whined about having been looking for those, for which he received a glare but no harsher treatment from our mother, who took me by my hair and tugged me by it outside and across the yard. I don't remember what she said before locking me in the chicken coop to think about my behavior.

I'm sure sin was spread as generously in her speech as bacon grease was in her cooking.

When I was let back in—everyone else had already eaten—I was given a turkey and a talking-to on the natural order between men and women. I wasn't hungry, but not finishing would lead to a speech on ungratefulness, so I swallowed every bite of stuffing, wishing I could hide with the chickens whose clucking I couldn't have understood had it been hateful.

"Kitty! The foam is overflowing!"

Switching to the present, I flipped the switch on the machine, swearing as milk spilled over the sides and burned my fingers. Sissy started wiping the foam from the floor. Emily shoved my hands under cold water, asking what was wrong with me, which I insisted was nothing, that I'd merely been distracted a moment.

"Darlin', your shirt's stained. Go change."

"I don't have a clean one."

"Go get one of mine. Then bring your laundry down."

While she started sharing some anecdote from my childhood with Sissy, I shut the door behind me as I entered Emily's room, strangely satisfied with the solitude of the walk-in closet that held more shoes and shirts than I'd owned in a lifetime, some costing more money than I earned on a sale from a single painting.

Slipping my shirt off and realizing the bra was soaked, I unclipped it, wiping my skin clean with the shirt so as not to mess up one of Emily's towels. As I pulled a shirt from a hanger, I noticed a stack of leather-bound notebooks I'd assumed she would have thrown away when cleaning Eleanor's room. As I picked one up and flipped through the pages, I recognized Emily's looped cursive and the brightness of semi-fresh ink.

I miss Eleanor more than ever now that Kitty's here, but it's different. Before, I felt so alone, and now, even though she spends most of her time painting, and even when she's with me, she's lost in her own head, my life has purpose again.

She hasn't changed since she was a girl. In some ways she's regressed to the way she was before Eleanor's death, before they went to college, when she was a little girl afraid of her own feelings.

I clapped the notebook shut, searching through the stack for seven years ago.

Wrapping the diary in my messy shirt, I rushed upstairs, shoving the notebook into a drawer in my studio before bringing the laundry basket down.

"Can you manage yourself? Or do you need me to show you how?" Emily teased.

"I can do it. Sissy, do you have any laundry?"

"It's in the basket."

"Oh."

I glanced down at the mixed pile of clothes, my face flushing as, fighting the echo of the last line of the diary entry, I pressed my lips into Sissy's.

Sissy stumbled back as I pulled away, smiling as I disappeared into the laundry room.

I overheard giggles and Emily saying something about making me do laundry more often. I blocked their words out as I threw the clothes into the machine.

It wasn't until the cycle finished that I realized I'd forgotten to add detergent.

Though it is a cliché to say, there are few times during which I have been as thankful as I was that Thursday while we were gathered around the table. As the sun began to set, Emily and I shifted from chardonnay to Beaujolais. Sissy and I scooted closer to each other, our hands intertwining while the cork popped from the bottle, our lips touching as Emily poured the wine into fresh glasses.

"You taste like butter," Sissy said, and I answered it was the wine. Since it was the only wine she could get, Sissy sucked at my lips again so hard that Emily told her to stop.

"I won't have you learn bad manners in my home," Emily scolded.

I answered, "You're the one always telling me to not be so shy about my feelings."

"When have I ever said that?"

As she sipped, I spotted one of Eleanor's smirks. I downed a quick gulp as I ran through my movements in Emily's closets, hoping she wouldn't notice if I had mixed up the order of the diaries or left one eschew.

"Nevertheless," Emily continued after her first sip, "I am very thankful both of you are here. This has been the best Thanksgiving in years. By far."

Her grin was earnest, and I saw hints of tears forming in the corners of her eyes. She seemed ready to give a speech, but before she could begin, a rumbling carried over from a distance. Sipping her wine, Emily looked over her shoulder as Sissy and I leaned past to see a run-down truck rolling over the dirt road, its thick tires bouncing over the gravel.

Sissy's fingers tightened around mine.

"Stay here," I told her, standing as her father stepped out of the car, chugging the last drops of a whiskey bottle.

I went to the door, descending the first few steps as he tossed the empty bottle to the ground, pointing his fingers at me as his head swung from side to side, gripping the side of his car and nearly slipping. "Give me back my daughter, you slut!"

"Daddy, go home!" Sissy shouted from behind me.

"You're comin' with me!"

I took a few steps towards the car. "You need to leave, Mr. Evergreen. I'll call you a cab, and I'll pay for it."

"Tryin' to buy her for yourself like last time?" His feet stumbled under him.

"I'll drive you home," I offered.

"Not unless she's comin'! That's my grandchild she's got! And it ain't your baby!"

I took in a heavy breath. "No, it's hers. And she's chosen to live here."

In a flash, a gun was pointed at my chest.

Gasping, I took a step back, holding up my hands. "Put the gun down, please. We can sit down and talk about this."

"There ain't nothin' to talk about!"

He unclicked the safety. Sissy screamed, and he shifted his aim from me to her. "Wicked child!" he spat, "Worse than your mama. Have I not fed you for eighteen years? Given you a roof over your head?"

"Daddy, put the gun down, please! I'll come if you just put it down!"

"You're lyin'."

He narrowed his eyes, fixing his aim.

A shot rang out, echoing as far as the edges of the ranch.

Sissy's father fell by my feet.

"Sissy, go call 911," Emily said as she reloaded the shotgun, but Sissy had started to puke.

He'd been shot in the leg, and the side of his car and the dirt was being stained red as he struggled in his own pool of blood.

He fired his gun, but the bullet skimmed the side of his truck.

Emily pulled her cell phone out of her pocket, tossing it to me. It fell on the ground, and I scrambled to pick it up, frantically trying to figure out the code and settling for the emergency call button as Sissy's father struggled to point his gun.

"I'll shoot!" he shouted as she approached him step by step.

"Go ahead. Death row'll be waiting," Emily threatened.

"You won't kill me."

"You ain't heard what I do when animals hurt my girls," Emily said, aiming.

The operator asked me what my emergency was. I don't know how I managed the words Rosewood and guns.

"Please," the man started to cry, his hands shaking as he raised his gun to his own head.

Emily didn't flinch, but she didn't tell him not to do it.

"Daddy! Don't!" Sissy cried, and I caught her as she tried to fling herself towards him.

"Kitty, take her inside," Emily ordered.

I tried, but she squirmed out of my arms, running towards them.

Her father lowered the gun from his head, but just as it inched, maybe in our direction, Emily fired.

CHAPTER TWENTY

D eath, even when desired, distant, or necessary, feels dirty.

Despite the wine from dinner and whiskey that followed death, I didn't permit my stone-cold resolve to slip, not during the police interrogations. The officers seemed satisfied by our testaments. My devotion to detail – the pinkish color the blood had been before it became brown – the stench of gunpowder fresh from the barrel – the taste of vomit as it starts low in your stomach and rises slowly from one intestine to the next and up and out through your esophagus – was probably unnecessary and dismissed as excessive artistic detail.

We scheduled a visit to the police station next week for formal statements. For now, we were told, with awkwardly sympathetic smiles, to enjoy our holiday as though a man had not just been killed in our driveway and though one of us had not killed him, as though he had not been one of our fathers.

It was a clear-cut case of self-defense, so they said.

Everyone in the area knew Danny Evergreen was a drunk, and Emily was a sympathetic character if not an upstanding citizen. Plus, she'd paid for the county's new hospital wing.

Sissy went to bed as soon as Emily and I returned home.

Given her pregnancy and shock, Sissy had been spared questioning. It only occurred to me later that Sissy had said her ex-boyfriend's father was the sheriff

He'd given no indication of any familiarity with Sissy or any affection towards a potential grandchild, making me wonder if he knew. Either way, I suspect that his apathy made Sissy feel even more alone following the departure of her own father.

After Sissy went upstairs, Emily shakily poured more whiskey.

She moved as though walking through film, having answered the police's questions dryly while drinking like her liver was steel and people were props to be addressed as she moved about a set that had altered itself without her knowing while she still remembered the blocking.

Even at Eleanor's funeral, she had seemed less like a ghost, but based on the blankness I felt in my own mind, I suspected she felt the same when she looked at me.

For Sissy, Emily and I had held our heads firm with the police, but now, neither one of us knew which one needed to be strong for the other. Since I was a girl, she'd been strong for me. But she was no longer the goddess on the pedestal of my youth and there was a young, pregnant woman who desperately needed both of us to be more mature than any woman honestly could be.

I sat beside my maternal idol-turned-murderess on the couch, watching golden-brown liquid swish around the inside of my glass. It was her most expensive Bourbon, and if there's ever been a time to drink it, it was now, though even as the harsh liquid stung the sides of my esophagus, I knew that no whiskey, no matter the cost, could cure us.

The glass clinked as I set it on the coffee table. I shoved my face into my hands, preemptively rubbing away the headache I knew the morning would bring, but it wasn't that late, and I wasn't yet drunk, and my mind was so resolute I sensed that, no matter how much whiskey we had, my senses would stay sharp.

"I've never seen someone die," Emily whispered, her tone as monotone as when she'd answered the police, except now her voice was quiet, intimate.

Running my hands through my hair and pulling my head up from my hands, I shifted my neck to look at her.

She seemed to have aged ten years since the morning, but at the same time, it was like I was looking at a little girl.

"I've never killed anything, either. Except bugs."

Thomas had shot the bull that killed Eleanor. Emily had shot the beast until there was hardly anything left of it and smashed it with the butt of the shotgun until police pulled her away, but she hadn't taken its life.

Even with the image of her mutilating an animal so vivid in my mind, it had been impossible for me to imagine Emily breaking into violence fit for a horror film. But that bull had been dead but a beast.

Sissy's father, despite having a soul darker than an animal's, had been a human being, not a dumb creature that had itself been a victim of Eleanor's madness. Yet, in my mind, Daniel Evergreen hadn't been worthy of the quick death the bullet granted.

"You saved Sissy's life, and maybe mine," I reassured her, though we both were certain of the uncertainty of this fact. We thought the gun had been pointed at Sissy or me, but maybe it had been a drunken twitch or a movement made in pain.

"I don't regret it," Emily mused, sipping whiskey between thoughts. "Yet even though he was older than me, I can't help but be grateful that his mother's already dead. I don't know how I would face her." Her head shook, shoulders shrugged as she sipped. "I suppose I'll have to in hell."

"You're not a murderer."

"Even so," she admitted, "There's plenty of other things I'm going for. I'll have to face him, too."

"You'll be in different circles."

"As long as I'm with Eleanor, it doesn't matter."

"Don't kill yourself!" I insisted, fearing where the whiskey was taking her.

"No. I couldn't do that. I thought about it after Eleanor died. More than I'd care to admit."

I picked up my whiskey, thinking the same but unable to admit it.

I let the whiskey burn down my throat.

"Kitty?"

I swallowed, setting the glass down.

She was fighting her tears, and when I thought of all the tears she must have been holding, my heart ripped. I outstretched my arms, letting her fall into them, rubbing her back as she shook and whispering that it was alright as she said she was sorry and sorry, sorry for me, sorry for the portrait, sorry for Sissy's father and sorry for crying, sorry that all she wanted was her mother.

A tear trickled as I imagined my own mother in her oversized garden, surrounded by my siblings and her grandchildren but without me, outwardly disowning me for my lack of religion and respect for whatever excuse she could find, all the while inwardly wishing she could shrink me down to my infant size and cuddle me in her arms, quietly yearning as Emily did now to be swaddled and to swaddle.

I thought of Sissy, of how she must have constantly coveted affection that was nowhere to be found, of where her mother must be, constantly regretting having left or ambivalently having forgotten her daughter, of how come summer, Sissy would have her own child after whose admiration she would forever be striving, all the while searching for her own standing as a woman without having grown up with one to guide her.

I held Emily close, and as her hands clutched at my arms, her body shaking in violent sorrow, I understood what I had to do.

My eyes closed, and I pictured Eleanor.

At first, she taunted me, scoffing at her mother's weakness and criticizing me for encouraging it. But then I stared back, glaring until she respected my resolve.

I kissed her mother's head and told her that it was time for bed.

If she hadn't been so tall, I would have carried her. As it was, she became somewhat conscious of her position as she rose from my arms, wiping her tears and looking around the room as though she'd stepped out of her movie. She was so tired that she was already halfway into the world of dreams.

I rubbed her back, and she kissed my cheek. Then she headed off to her room for what I hoped would be peaceful dreams.

When she was gone, I put away the whiskey, wine, and dishes, wiped the table, and turned on the dishwasher. I went through the actions I'd seen Emily perform hundreds of times without giving them a second thought, beginning to comprehend how lonely the mundane tasks of motherhood must have been.

At least my mother had my father, and once, Emily had had Thomas, but when had I ever seen either of those men stay up late and clean up after the mess they'd help make?

Sissy would have no husband to complain to, only a rapist to complain about.

She'd have me, I thought as I flicked off the light and snuck up the stairs in the dark, careful not to let the wood creak under the weight of my feet.

When I crawled into bed, I drew my body as close as I could to Sissy's without waking her, trying to make out her face in the dark and discover what dreams she might have been experiencing.

Eventually, my eyes closed on their own as I waited for morning, rising as though a thread had been strung from sleeping to waking. Before falling asleep, I had wondered if my resolution would waver, but it awoke stronger than when it had first formed in my head.

I waited with more patience than I knew I possessed for Sissy to wake, cherishing the gentleness of her breaths and innocence of her sleep, mourning the future and the fact that in less than nine months, an infant's cries would wake her.

She stirred, stretching her limbs as she always did, as though trying to steal my feline nickname, blinking at me through half-awake eyes. I stole a kiss before she could open them all the way, feeling fuzzy with warmth as she snuggled into my embrace.

After a few long, sleepy kisses, she crawled on top of me. I was tempted to let her continue rolling her kisses along the length of my body, but I blurted out what I wanted to say.

"I want to adopt the baby."

She straightened, tilting her head to the side, and then she slumped, taking my hands in hers and twisting my fingers in her palms.

"I want to keep it," she answered quietly. I contorted my limbs so my lips could reach hers as combed through her scalp down to her split ends.

"I want that, too, but you're so," I kissed her, my words getting caught in the sadness in her eyes, "so young."

"It's my baby."

"You're just a baby."

She opened her mouth to protest, but I kissed her.

"A sweet, beautiful, crazily mature baby, but still a baby." I sighed, searching for sentences to express my wisdom without isolating her. You've lived more than your share of struggles, but that's all the more reason why you should be free. Don't you dream of going to college? Of running to catch night trains in Europe? Or staying up partying until the sun rises? You haven't even begun to live."

"And you have?"

"More than I wish."

My forehead rested against hers as one of my hands fell to her stomach.

I tried to picture the baby within, thinking of Sissy's bright eyes on a chubby infant face coupled with her playful grin.

"The only person I have ever come close to loving as much as I love you is dead," I admitted. However, a part of me whispered to myself that it was a lie, that I'd loved Lana Lane with similar fervor, that once or twice another woman, and for a single second, even a man had sent my heart skipping to that same beat. "You take on this baby on your own, your life will be over in seven years. Your heart might be beating and your body still moving, but this spark within you will be gone."

Her head fell to my shoulder.

"You don't have to decide today," I reassured her.

"But I'll need to decide soon."

"Your father just died. You deserve some time."

"I would need you to do something," she said, rubbing her nose over the veins in my neck.

"Anything," I promised.

But she asked for the one thing I didn't want to happen, though we knew it was what needed to happen, even if I wasn't going to be a mother.

"You need to get rid of your ghost."

CHAPTER TWENTY-ONE

Touch is its own type of ghost, a medium of a feeling held within our hearts, an apparition of all that our souls cannot quite say.

Yet to try and touch the souls of the dead is one of the greatest of evils. Even touching their bodies is taboo.

Merely setting eyes upon the bodies of the dead is supposed to make our stomachs spin. But the corpse of Daniel Evergreen didn't sicken me as the battered but breathing body of his daughter had when I'd rescued her from his clutches.

I understood, as I looked upon his cleaned, botoxed, and powdered forehead, how Emily had beaten the body of the bull that had killed Eleanor.

He didn't deserve to be buried in a coffin and a suit and wasn't worthy of the headstone and funeral that Emily paid for. I couldn't criticize her for that. Her grief was her own, separate yet intertwined from Sissy's and mine.

The funeral wasn't crowded, but not because of the pandemic. There hadn't been people who cared about him.

There was no one except Sissy and me to sit in the front row. Emily kept herself to the back, though as the funeral home was nearly empty, her self-isolation was unnecessary for everyone except her.

No one spoke except the minister, and even he struggled to find praise for the man, having managed to find a few anecdotes from long, long ago.

The man described seemed stock from a storybook. Sissy twitched as she struggled to recognize the character being built from stereotypes.

We didn't hold a wake. The burial was quick, the dirt having barely left our hands before we walked away, but as we reached the edge of the graveyard, Sissy stopped, dropping my hand.

"I want to say goodbye. Alone."

We nodded, letting her go back as we waited by the chapel, looking out upon the rows of headstones.

In the third plot on the right, Eleanor was buried.

Even from our distance, the angel statue stuck up over the rows of plain, curved cement graves.

Emily hated it, but Thomas had insisted.

Eleanor would have despised it.

She'd told me once she would have been content to be dumped in a mass, unmarked grave and forgotten to history. Then she had decided she wanted to decompose and have a tree planted over her but occasionally mused about a Viking-style burial in a burning boat. If she'd been honest, only a mausoleum with a terracotta army could have met her standards.

Around the cemetery, my family was scattered, primarily people who'd died before I could remember them or whose memories were but half-formed apparitions of a family from a nearly forgotten past.

In the end, these bodies were dead, their skins rotted, yet when I picked up a handful of their dust, I rarely thought that I might be holding the minerals that had made up saints, that the cells of sinners didn't differ from the saved.

On that day, if only for a second so small that a clock might not have ticked, I saw for the first time that the dirt from Eleanor's flesh was the same as the rest.

Even from our distance, I heard Sissy sobbing at her father's grave.

My bones called out in desperation to hold her, unsatisfied that they had to settle for Emily, whose stability had been restored, leaving no taints of the girl who'd broken down in my arms except within my whiskey-stained memory. Now, whenever I looked at Emily, I saw her hiding within the folds of her heart, and her weakness made the woman who dressed up for the funeral of the man she'd killed all the more magnificent.

I'd never asked Emily if I could photograph her, but nothing could have made her more complete than capturing her in her dark, wide-brimmed hat and black dress. Except that, no matter how high-quality the image turned out, no one except me would see the true Emily.

She caught me admiring her, and she smiled, slightly embarrassed but mostly flattered as she always was whenever anyone complimented her.

I looked away as though ashamed by her charm, but as soon as I did, I caught Eleanor's reaction peeking over from her grave.

She would have been bitter, first at her mother's beauty, then at me for acknowledging it, and then angry at her mother for being flattered and annoyed with me for being ashamed. She could never let those subtle, secret exchanges go unnoticed, and now, neither could I.

Ghosts couldn't be killed, only chased away, and I feared I might never chase Eleanor away even though I promised, because I wasn't sure I wanted to. For years, grief had been my drug, but even before she'd died, I'd been addicted. When I'd loved Lana and those other women, and when Sissy entered my life, it occurred to me that loving her might only be like replacing whiskey with wine.

Yet she didn't trap me the way Eleanor had. She freed me.

My head fell on Emily's shoulder while we waited, averting our eyes to grant Sissy privacy.

I thought of asking if she wanted to visit Eleanor's grave. I even thought of showing it to Sissy, but instead, I asked Emily if she'd walk with me to my grandparents' plots.

They'd never meant much to me, but their blood flowed within my veins along with the other Kunz and Hinze ashes scattered throughout the yard.

My ancestors on both sides had left the Old World in the mid-nineteenth century. Between them and me, not a single generation had settled outside of the Texas Hill Country. Once, I'd been determined to be the first. Thus far, I'd made it the farthest, even returned to our ancestral homeland as I crossed the pond from new to old, only to return and find what I had thought was new was even more ancient than the nightclubs in Berlin and the fluorescent U-Bahn signs scattered around Vienna.

Being connected to the ground beneath one's feet was a sensation seldom felt in a world in which we moved as fleetingly as flies. I was desperate for my child to feel the ground stably beneath their toes if Sissy would allow it.

My eyes only skimmed the graves of my ancestors for long enough to feel I'd fulfilled an obligation. As soon as I told myself I would replace the flowers while knowing I never would, I went back to watching Sissy.

I had yet to lose a parent, so I had no right to presume what she might have felt, but as I watched her weep for a man she'd hated, I began to comprehend the significance of this loss.

Her child would have neither grandparents nor a father.

Our child, or even my child, if she would allow it, and if she did, then one day I would bring that child to this very place. We would bury Emily, and hopefully, Sissy and that child would bury me, and years from now, that child and our descendants might lean down and pick up a pile of this Texan dust and think of me.

There was a gap between May 12 and 20, the day before the funeral, but I glossed over this, not knowing what I sought until I found it.

The drugs and drinks only make it worse.

Her handwriting was shaky, and mistakes were scattered throughout.

Only when I take so much that the world goes dark can I escape her. Then the hangover is so stiff I can't imagine doing it again. But I do, sometimes with Thomas, but usually alone.

We hate each other.

Last night, or early this morning, or maybe the night before, all the days scrambled in my head, he started choking me so hard during sex that I couldn't breathe, but I didn't ask to stop.

I forced him to come inside me. I never do that, even though it's too late to get pregnant.

After he did, I wouldn't let him leave me, and I forced him to eat me.

It was all so intense I don't know if I ever came, and at some point I don't remember anything.

I drew the cover hanging over Eleanor's portrait.

From Emily's words, I painted Eleanor, letting colors synthesize with syllables as her punctuation became brushstrokes and her phrases my frame as from sentences formed skin.

CHAPTER TWENTY-THREE

S ince I returned to working in spurts and sleeping in my studio, it was clear to Sissy and Emily that I'd resumed Eleanor's portrait and set aside my self-portrait.

The magazine kept me from going completely crazy and keeping my promise to Sissy that I would rid myself of my ghost. I needed money, and though the deadline for the next issue was months away, I needed to review submissions.

For months, I'd avoided viewing others' work so as not to distract from my own, which meant a pile awaited me.

Painting was immersive, and the slightest distraction drew me out of my work. The littlest of influences could compel me to destroy an entire piece.

To prevent cross-contamination of ideas, I shut away Eleanor's portrait when I wasn't working on it, altering my headspace for the magazine with music not even remotely related to anything Eleanor would have listened to or what I would have under ordinary circumstances. I don't think I even enjoyed the music, but it helped me work.

Most of the magazine's submissions were bad, but my standards were too high, and as the staff constantly commented, my standards were strange and inconsistent.

During my residency in London, I made logos for companies on the side, and the commercially-centered mundanity drove me crazy. I couldn't stand the drive for cash and capitalism's deduction of art to consumerism. Even more than that, I detested the commonplace, ready-made covers claiming to be cosmopolitan that stocked kiosk counters.

My past girlfriends and flings hadn't understood my craving to separate myself from these products, never shown an interest in the avant-garde magazines I worked for, but Sissy interrupted me so often with questions that it was endearing until it became so annoying I had to put her to work to keep her from bothering me, coming up with copy editing tasks that, as she completed them so eagerly, reminded me of our age difference as well as what had first drawn me to her.

Her eyes glistened when she looked at the pictures. I could almost hear her heart beating faster when an article excited her or she discovered a better way of phrasing something.

"My father never understood me," Sissy confessed as she and I sorted submissions.

I wanted to admit that mine didn't, either, to say we shared this division between the world into which we were born and the one we chose. But I lacked the courage to share my feelings even with her.

Art has been an escape from many things, from violence and sadness, boredom, school, Eleanor, and my family. It had been the most incredible escape. Even when they burned my sketchbooks because of their indecency, art had emerged within my only safe space, my mind.

It was, I realized as Sissy spoke, the reason I had never painted my family.

Sharing this with Sissy would have brought us closer, but I was forced to share my sorrow for Eleanor with Emily. My family was a sadness I wished to keep to myself. I suspected Sissy felt the same about her father, so we continued to silently sort, and when we went to sleep, we said nothing except for Sissy's statement that she was too tired for sex and my ambivalent comment about not being in the mood.

Christmas was soon, so one morning, Emily asked what I thought we should do. Considering Thanksgiving concluded with a shoot-out, none of us were keen to discuss the next holiday.

I answered by saying I hadn't really thought about it.

"I'm getting Sissy a car," she said.

"Whatever I get her will be much smaller. And cheaper," I laughed, adding, "You don't need to get me anything."

"Don't worry. I will," she teased, and we settled on having a small dinner and exchanging gifts. "Tomorrow I'm riding the perimeter of the property. I do it once a month. Will you come with me?"

"It's been ages since I've been on a horse," I resisted, but Emily was persistent.

"Don't worry. We'll go slow."

We started slow, but as we got going, it was like being on a bike for the first time in years, and I was eager for speed.

Despite it being December and several degrees cooler than the month prior, the sun still shone harshly through midday, making us delay our departure to late afternoon.

As we rode, Emily told me the number of acres and spat off details about the size of the property. They sounded big but without a frame of reference were like nonsense. The only way to make sense of Rosewood was to spend hours in a saddle and ride across stretches of vast open space.

There was magic in Rosewood, spells rooted in its history and scenery.

A few miles from the house but still on the property were remnants of a church from the Spanish times, and scattered about were pieces of the past that were so picturesque they were almost pleading to be forgotten and lost to the sunset. It was so exquisitely Texan that there were constant requests to film Westerns.

None of the requests were granted, not even the one for the film that had made Lana Lane a star, the most famous and stereotypical cowgirl flick of all time, perhaps because it was one of the only.

The Pontell family needed neither the money nor the attention, and when Lana Lane visited after becoming a star, she had remarked that Rosewood never would have suited Hollywood.

"It's too real," had been her exact words.

Yet, as we reached the highest point of the property, Rosewood seemed anything but that.

"Let's take a break," Emily suggested, and as we dismounted our horses, she pulled out a flask.

"Don't tell me you just come out here every month to drink," I teased.

"Just when someone's with me," she grinned.

I lifted the flask to my lips and let the liquid roll around my tongue and down my throat, shaking my head as my insides burned.

"What is that?"

When she sipped, she made a face, but her reaction wasn't as violent as mine. "Mezcal. Too strong?"

"Too smoky."

She took another swig and handed it back. I braced myself before the second sip.

When I looked back, I saw her mind was far away. I knew Eleanor was always on her mind, and when she was in Eleanor's memory, the insides of her eyes softened as the muscles around them hardened, the corners of her lips curving up while the centers tightened. Then she'd cross her arms, and inevitably, her palm fell over her chest.

"I think I was in love with Rosewood more than I was in love with my husband," she admitted as her eyes fixed on the house.

"You grew up in a great house," I reminded her.

The Chopin family was just as old and even prouder than the Pontell. They could trace their lineage from beyond the Canadian expulsion to France to some chateau in Aquitaine, from whose ancient queen Eleanor had become a traditional family name, though up through Emily's mother, the traditional French Alienor had always been used. Emily claimed she'd anglicized it for her daughter at Thomas's behest, but Emily had never bent to Thomas's will except in agreeing to change her own name from Chopin to Pontell. I wondered if the rejection of her mother's name stemmed from a desire to please or the necessity of separation, for Rosewood could not incorporate another family or language other than its own.

Rosewood could only ever be Rosewood.

"I did," Emily conceded," but it never felt like home, not after coming here. Not once Eleanor was born."

I knew the story of Emily Chopin's childhood and heard how she fell in love with Thomas and became Emily Pontell, though that was a tale I'd only heard from him. The stories from her childhood were pieced together, and she never brought them up. Her relatives had sometimes visited, and I'd tagged along on their annual trip to Louisiana since Eleanor hated these excursions and needed a distraction. Emily appeared to enjoy the trips and displayed a fondness for the home in which she'd come of age, but she was never sad to leave.

Her family had always been distant. Her father died when she was in college, her mother during her infancy, and the way I'd heard her father described it was hard to imagine Emily's childhood as warm. She'd grown up an only child on an estate that, though smaller than Rosewood, was more than most people dreamed of owning. She had cousins, and after her father's death, she let them live in the house, which, by the state's strange inheritance laws, belonged partially to them anyway. When she'd shown me her old bedroom that had been transformed into an office, she didn't bat an eye.

"I grew up a daughter without a mother, and now I'm a mother without a daughter," Emily said as she looked from Rosewood to me. "Sissy told me you want to adopt the baby."

"But you think Sissy should keep the baby," I said.

"No. She's not ready for that, but she should stay close. Both of you should."

"Close to what?"

She nodded to the house, reaching into the back pocket and unfolding a piece of paper before handing it to me. "It's a copy of Eleanor's will."

"I didn't know she made a will."

"She didn't want you to. At least not until some time had passed."

"It says that?"

"No. She wrote me a letter."

"You said she didn't leave a note."

"She didn't. She wrote me a letter."

I wanted to ask more, but Emily pointed to a paragraph.

During the divorce, Emily and Thomas had preemptively ceded Rosewood to Eleanor. I assumed they had inherited it jointly and that when Thomas died, there were no heirs except Emily.

Until their deaths, Thomas Joseph Pontell and Emily Ruth Pontell shall remain in possession of Rosewood and its estate. They cannot sell it or do anything that would diminish its value. Upon their deaths, Katherine Naomi Kunz shall be the sole proprietor of Rosewood.

CHAPTER TWENTY-FOUR

I turned off.

My heartbeat and blood flowed through my veins. My brain functioned, ordering my nerves to register touch and taste to complete the tasks within the timeframes I'd set for myself. The final selections for the magazine were made. Christmas presents bought, for Emily a vintage country music record set, for Sissy a journal I realized while wrapping was the same brand and color as Emily's, an artifact that remained untouched since the revelation of my inheritance.

I'd told Sissy the news about Rosewood, and when she asked how I felt, I answered that I wasn't ready to talk about it.

As I held the copy of the will, fresh from Emily's hands, I hadn't said a word, not even to excuse her apologies for keeping it from me nor to answer if I were alright.

"I just want to go home," I'd said, and as I stepped through the oversized doors, the word took on a new meaning.

Rosewood was not mine yet, but it would be one day, and for the past seven years had existed in this would-be state without me ever knowing it.

Now, I was more careful with the dishes and noticed new details in the design, pointing out to Emily that the trim on the curtains didn't match. She asked if I wanted it changed, as though the decision were mine. I said whatever, but the next day, they were replaced.

Without telling Sissy or Emily, I put in my notice at the magazine. It would be my final issue.

If Rosewood were to be mine, why worry about the scraps of money my salary offered?

Eleanor's portrait was left covered in the corner, and I didn't allow myself to entertain the idea of working on it.

On Christmas morning, I programmed my mind to concentrate only on the holiday, starting by cherishing the morning with Sissy. We'd set no alarm, but I woke at the hour I always did. Without a ringing to bother her into rolling over, I admired her expression as she slept, noticing that her cheeks had put on weight, as had the rest of her body as, bit by bit, her pregnancy began to show.

When she woke, my hand was resting on her stomach. My mind was morning-dreaming of a toddler rolling in the fields and racing me to the creek as Eleanor. I had romped about without caring for anyone or anything except ourselves.

"Merry Christmas," she whispered.

I kissed her stomach. "Merry Christmas."

"Which one of us are you talking to?"

"I can talk to both of y'all at the same time," I answered, lifting my head and bringing my lips to hers. We kissed for some time before settling back into bed. I said a few things about how it was always dark during Christmas in Vienna.

I wondered if Hélène was still in France at her mother's or if she'd found another lover. I also wondered how Lana and her girls were celebrating, thinking that in Europe, it was already evening and their presents would already be torn open, their carols already sung and egg nogg already empty.

I hadn't had Christmas with my family since I was a child, so I couldn't picture being there, but I guessed it was as chaotic as all other holidays.

The butter my mother had thrown into the shopping cart before Thanksgiving crossed my mind, and I thought about what she might have baked.

"Do you miss your father?" I asked Sissy.

"Would you miss yours?"

I searched my mind for happy memories of home, so distant and clouded that I couldn't enjoy them. However, there had been five years of my life before I met Eleanor, and even in my early years with her, I couldn't have hated my family, but that didn't mean I'd loved them.

"I want you to have the baby."

"What?" I asked, looking up. I hadn't pressed her on the subject again, so this statement seemed to come from nowhere.

"You should be the mother."

I stroked the side of her cheek. "You'll always be the mother. You're doing the hard work."

"Just for nine months. Then the hard work is yours."

"I don't think raising a child is anything like your pain."

"It's probably worse, and it isn't over after nine months."

"You don't want to do it together?"

"You're the one who said I should be free."

"I know I think you should be, but I also want you to stay."

"I will. At least next year. Then I want to go to college in New York. Like you did."

I grinned, kissing her. "You'll love New York."

Again, we kissed, prolonging, leaving the warmth of each other's arms. With this conversation came a thousand others. Who would legally hold custody? What would happen to us? We chose to wait to address these topics, gifting ourselves a day with each other, with our hopes and dreams. When we went downstairs and found a colorful Christmas tree with stuffed stockings, our childhood selves escaped, and we began ripping wrapping paper and littering the floor.

Emily laughed at our indulgence but also let herself loose, playing the records as soon as she opened them.

I watched Emily as Sissy opened the journal, checking if it might reveal that I'd stolen a diary. Emily did, for a second, seem confused or disturbed, but the expression shifted soon. It was a familiar enough brand, albeit expensive.

We ate casserole after presents, a Pontell tradition and as we ate, Emily switched the country records for Christmas ones. Occasionally, one of us would hum along, but mostly, we chatted. I told stories of Christmas in Europe, smiling as Sissy's eyes brightened at the subject of snow, so Emily and I told tales of our trips to Telluride and Taos, where the Pontells and I had gone back in the day.

Sissy didn't share magical memories, but that made the day all the more magical because we knew this day was the first Christmas to live up to the fantasies forged by carols and classic films.

After we ate, we gathered around the table for a game of cards, and I discovered Sissy's competitive side. She showed her frustration when she played, unlike Emily, who was merciless and devious while never showing it. I was ambivalently amused.

"I need to walk," I said, stretching my arms as it became mid-afternoon. The pie and ham had caught up to me, and sitting made me stiff. Emily and Sissy stayed and played while I went to wander.

I wasn't sure where I was walking to, only that I needed to.

The grass rubbed my heels, and as the blades itched at my skin, I watched Eleanor lean down to whack at a bug, listening to her complain about the heat. The farther I walked, the more she came back, her words evolving from single phrases to complete sentences and speeches, and my visions of isolated movements pieced together to form a whole woman walking with me, side by side, across the field, her hand clasping mine as we reached the barn.

Goats nibbled at the grass, glared at me, then lowered their necks to the ground again.

As I touched the chipping paint of the barn, she kissed me.

The world stood still, but I span, or maybe it was the other way around, that I kissed and dizzied her, or both, since with Eleanor, I was in the whole world but nowhere with and in her, within and without as when her lips vanished, I was alone except for the nagging of goats and rustling of the wind, and, so far away I feared it was disappearing with Eleanor, music.

As I approached the house, the song became recognizable alongside the slightly out-of-tune piano keys.

Sissy sat by the fireplace, her eyes lifting from the hand on her stomach to me, smiling as I went to Emily and rested a hand on her shoulder while she continued to play.

When the carol looped back to the beginning, I sang. As words and notes escaped, my soul awoke again, my body and heart igniting every inch that had been turned off, and once all bits of me were on again, I broke.

CHAPTER TWENTY-FIVE

I wish I'd been given the gift of breaking, of mourning the me who was not knowingly the heiress of Rosewood, of facing my ghost, and of finishing the portrait, but as I was painting, only a few days after Christmas when I had permitted myself a break down, Emily interrupted. The hesitant way she moved while she instructed me to sit prevented me from complaining.

As she opened her mouth, she stopped herself, glancing around as though to find a reason to prolong her news. The mess would have been a good excuse. My heartbeat escalated at the thought that she might open the drawer and find her diary. Still, then she told me my mother was dead, and the broken part of me switched off again.

"Your sister called," Emily explained, adding a few incomprehensible and unnecessary details about when and where exactly she'd picked up the phone, as though to give me time to process or grant her own words the authority necessary to express death. She died last night. Your mother, not your sister. Covid, but she was apparently diabetic, too. She had some other health issues. She refused to go to the hospital until it was too late. Your sister was with her."

I set my brush in a cup of water, stirring it until the liquid darkened. "I didn't know she was sick," I said.

"She didn't want you to. At least that's what your sister said."

"Seems everyone is keeping secrets from me until they die."

"I'm not."

"No, you're just keeping the dead's secrets."

I waited, though I wasn't sure for what. *An apology, maybe?* I thought as I removed the brush from the water and dried the smooth, slick bristles. More sympathy? To be alone? Another secret to be revealed? I hadn't meant to accuse her of anything. I hadn't had the chance to fully process the news about Rosewood, and hearing about my mother's death opened unexpected gateways in my heart.

I wouldn't ask Emily to apologize for keeping her daughter's secrets. She'd given me more sympathy than I deserved, and I didn't want to be alone, but for some reason, I said I did, so Emily left.

Though in my studio, I was never truly alone. Eleanor's bones might as well have been the ceiling and floor, her skin the walls.

Wallowing in my motherless state, I pulled up photographs I'd snapped when I was a girl, scrolled through computer files I'd forgotten existed, and opened albums Emily had saved from the days when I'd still used film. I even ventured into the realm of the internet.

I had obligatory professional accounts across social media platforms. The last time I opened them was before the pandemic. My sisters had profiles, and as I made my way through the condolences people had posted, I found images of a mother I hadn't known for the past seven years, but scrolling through the photos made me feel like I had.

She was active in her church. Everyone in her church looked and probably thought like her. They held can drives and soup kitchens, and her face brightened in pictures with grandchildren.

Then, I came across a profile with her name on it. There were no photographs, no posts, and she followed only one account: @kittykunz. I traced my thumb over the screen of her activity.

She'd liked every single post I'd ever made.

I pressed the power button.

The sun was shining, and she wouldn't have liked me sitting at a desk in such beautiful weather, so I went for a jog and, though she would have hated it, plugged my ears with electronic music.

Then, I showered, had dinner, and avoided the subject. When I went up to bed almost right after eating, Emily asked if I wouldn't stay up until midnight.

It was New Year's Eve.

"No," was all I said, and I fell asleep before Sissy came to bed, not dreaming.

When I woke, I drank my coffee, kissed Emily, and headed to the house that was the first thing I remember painting.

My grandmother was still alive when I'd painted it; she'd died right before my first year of school.

She'd been a painter, too.

Her skills were not those of a master or even of a talented artist. Her paintings wouldn't have sold for more than a few bucks at a garage sale, but when she sat down with a brush, her eyes lighted with luster, which, to me, made her more of an artist than the professional ones I knew.

The sunroom had been her studio, and I still remember how her oils had made it smell different than the other rooms in the house, where fatty kitchen smells managed to grease their way through the door hinges.

Early on, I decided I would do what she did and create something beautiful, so I painted our house.

I wanted the place I lived to become a beautiful place, or maybe in those days, I actually thought it was.

Aesthetically speaking, the house wasn't ugly.

For someone coming from out of state, our place could have been considered a ranch in its own right.

We would only dare to refer to it as a farm, and even this term we used rather reluctantly since we only possessed a few acres and a chicken coop.

My grandfather had built the house, and my father had been born and reared in it, and if he had his way, he'd probably die in it as his father and mother had.

Standing below its rafters I saw that, in some ways, it was not so different from Rosewood, only much smaller and much more crowded.

My oldest sister, baby in arms, was the only one to come outside and greet me.

She awkwardly tried to hand him to me as a welcome gesture, but as she did, I opened the backseat and pulled out a painting.

"I had this lying around. Consider it a Christmas present ... or a condolence gift."

"Oh, that's lovely, Katherine, thank you," she managed, but by the tilting of her head to the side, I could tell she was confused about what it was supposed to be. Smiling, we swapped the baby for the painting as she said she was sure they could find a place for it. I was surprised that, as I took the wiggling little boy, the future mother in me stirred, and I eagerly held him as close to me as possible, thrilled by the fact that we shared the same blood. He was innocent, and our relationship was not yet mingled with long-held resentments or hatreds.

I wasn't surprised by the lack of enthusiasm from the others my entrance garnered, but that didn't mean it didn't hurt, and if I hadn't still been turned off, I might have cried.

The fact that I hadn't been around so many people in a long time only added to my discomfort. I was glad that the pandemic was an excuse to keep a healthy distance from everyone.

In the center of my room sat my father, so silent he was loud.

When I entered, his hands clenched around the arms of his chair, and his sole response to my greeting was a gruff nod. My brothers and their children sat around him, and from the kitchen, I could hear my younger sister and sisters-in-law. One of the children asked who I was, and when my older sister introduced me, another kid blurted out that I was the lesbian aunt.

"Joe, that's rude," my sister hushed him, but another one whined that it was true. The bickering began, only briefly interrupted by my sister's exclamation that I'd brought a painting.

"That's supposed to be art?" one of the children laughed.

The baby began to fidget in my arms, and I shifted the way I held his weight, which only made things worse. As the other children argued, he began to cry, so I quickly returned him to his mother's arms, and as soon as he was in them, he hushed.

"See! She can't even hold a baby! Or paint!" one of the kids laughed, and I wish I'd stood up for myself, but under my father's heavy gaze, my head drooped.

"I'm sorry," my sister whispered under her breath. Then, louder, she told me to sit down and asked if I'd like anything to drink. I asked for an iced tea, and someone else offered to get it as my sister propped the painting up against a wall.

Small talk with my sister ensued, and she introduced me to the wives, husbands, and children I'd never met. Other than my youngest brother, who was still in college, I was the only one who was neither married nor engaged. There were three nieces and four nephews, only two of whom I'd met. None of my siblings had jobs I found remotely interesting, and their children all had ordinary hobbies.

Only one of my sisters-in-law worked.

"Sissy Evergreen is in my class," she offered awkwardly as she handed me my tea.

"Really? What subject?" I asked.

"English and history."

One of my brothers, a math teacher, added that she'd been in his geometry class a few years back.

"She's never mentioned that," I said, sipping tea so sweet I could feel cavities caving as I swallowed.

"It ain't right."

My grip on the glass tightened. They were the first words my father had said since I'd walked in.

"Living with that girl like that."

"I know she's younger than I am," I began but was interrupted.

"That's not what I mean."

My eyes dropped to the tea as I swirled the ice cubes with my straw.

"It's against the laws of nature. Against the laws of God."

I set down the glass and smoothed out my pants.

"Your mother was ashamed of you."

"Daddy!" my sister hissed, and I was thankful that my siblings' reactions were as uneasy as hers. Their expressions made it clear they agreed with him, but they wouldn't have said so to my face.

"This is my house. And I don't want sinners in my house."

"Everyone's a sinner!" My sister reminded him.

"Not like that we ain't!"

He hit me.

Not then, not as he sat there supposedly mourning my dead mother.

No, at that moment, he was too old, lazy, and fat to lift his pre-diabetic body from the armchair in which he'd been decaying for years, and I was grown up. His weight could overpower me, but he wouldn't be able to catch me, and what was the point if I was already grown up and out from under his thumb of control? He only had words to hurt me with now, but every syllable stung like the lash of his belt, bringing me back to hiding under my bed or being locked in the chicken coop.

Feeling smaller than I had then, I didn't say anything except to tell my sister she didn't need to defend me. It was alright. We weren't here to talk about my sexuality. We were gathered to mourn.

Eventually, our father settled down and leaned back into his chair, folding his hands over his stomach and falling back into silence so small talk could resume.

My sister asked about my travels, so I told her as much as I could about Europe without sounding presumptuous, which was hard considering the only time she'd ever traveled out of state was over the Oklahoma border to a casino, the only weekend in her life she'd allowed herself to break free from our family's conservatism.

When she wound up tipsy and making out with a stranger, she swore never to do it again, and within a year, she'd gotten married and pregnant.

"D'ya hear from Lana Lane any these days?" one of my brothers interrupted with a smirk. She'd been at Eleanor's funeral. He'd asked for her autograph then, literally during the sermon, but hadn't had any paper and slid her the obituary program.

"Sometimes," I answered.

"What's she up to?"

"Being a movie star."

Someone else asked what Emily Pontell had done with Rosewood. "Heard she's renovated. Fixed it all up. Got rid of them cattle and got some sheep."

"It's only right," someone else muttered, "after what that girl did."

The other laughed. "She always was crazy."

One of their wives gave them a sharp look. "Don't you go around speaking ill of the dead, crazy or not." At the same time, my sister whispered to them that Eleanor had been my friend.

"She was a bit more than that."

I don't know who said it, and I didn't argue against it since it was true. We had been more than friends. We'd been more to each other than this family was to me.

"And what is that Evergreen girl to ya?" my oldest brother asked. He sat separate from the rest of us, not in a big armchair like our father. He hadn't earned that right yet, but he would someday soon, and his mirrored posture of our father and mimicry of tone made sure everyone knew it.

Everyone knew what the answer was, so I didn't bother saying we were living in sin, which, no matter how politely or openly I said she was my girlfriend, was what they would hear. "If you must know, I'm adopting her baby."

Someone scoffed. Everyone else fell silent, and once they were, my brother teased, "Didn't know it was legal for a woman like you to do that."

"Why would it make a difference?" I asked

"Well, for starters, who's the father gonna be?"

"There won't be one."

"A child needs a father, especially if it's a boy."

"And if it's a girl that doesn't matter?"

"Not as much."

"And what if the father were dead? Would that ruin a child forever?"

"That's different. If you were a normal woman, you might find a man one day or have someone around who'd be a good influence. But since you ain't... well, how's the kid ever supposed to learn how to behave?"

"Because you learned how to behave from Daddy?"

I bit my tongue and quickly shoved my straw in my mouth to swallow a serving of sugary comfort. As it chilled down my throat, I could see my father's fingers curling around the edge of his armchair as he pulled himself out of his lazy position.

With no idea where the strength came from, I spoke before he could reach the edge of his seat.

"Because I think his narrow-minded and cruel parenting is what drove Eleanor Pontell insane, because I had no hesitations about loving her until someone beat the shit out of me for a simple kiss and I felt like I had to be with boys just to feel safe enough to sleep in my own bed at night. So, I don't care if you think I'm living in sin or a woman like me raising a child is wrong, but the last thing I would want is for a girl like me or Eleanor to kill herself, because letting that happen is a sin far worse than touching a vagina instead of a penis."

Afraid I would crawl back into my couch of shame, I didn't let the shock settle in and spat on.

"And my child, boy or girl, is going to grow up with a much better home than any of us did, because Eleanor Pontell left every piece of Rosewood to me, so y'all better get used to me being around town."

The chickens clucked, which, on the farm, was the equivalent of a pen dropping.

My father sunk back into the sofa, his eyes lingering on what would be the last look he'd ever have of his daughter.

Images of people are even less objective than the photographs we make in our minds. A stranger could look upon this snapshot of my father and see an old, lonely man who'd just lost his wife of nearly fifty years being rejected by his daughter, never seeing the truth of a man who was heartless enough to say to his own flesh and blood, "Get out of my house, and don't ever come back."

"Don't worry. I don't want to," I said, and as I stood, I told him the price at which I'd sold my last painting, offering to put him in touch with a dealer. I mentioned that if there were any old pieces that happened to be lying around, they would probably find a nice price for those, too, adding, "If my art isn't worth anything to you, it's at least worth some money.

CHAPTER TWENTY-SIX

W hile the dirt on my mother's grave was still wet, Sissy and Emily and I went to pay our respects. We didn't attend the funeral. When Emily suggested it, I said it would only lead to trouble, and that wasn't how I wanted my mother to be remembered. My siblings deserved to mourn in peace. And I had a bad record of disturbing funerals.

Between my mother and Sissy's father and the heaps of flowers Emily replenished at Eleanor and Thomas's graves on a regular basis, Emily practically employed the local florist.

It was a bit much, I thought as we stood before the wreaths and lilies hiding the freshly carved inscriptions on my mother's headstone, especially considering they weren't really for my mother but so that Emily could feel like she'd tried her best to make me feel better.

None of us said anything as we left our flowers by the grave, and we hadn't been standing too long when Sissy asked if I would mind if she went to her father's headstone. I nodded, squeezing her hand as she walked away.

"It feels a bit surreal to be standing here with you," I said when Emily and I were alone.

"Would you like me to go?" she asked.

I shook my head, dropping my head onto her shoulder. She wrapped an arm around me and kissed the top of my head.

"This isn't the way it should be," I murmured.

"No, darling, it's exactly the way it should be," she said, brushing hair aside from my face. "Trust me. No matter what was going on between you and your mother, she's glad that she went before you did."

"That's not what I meant," I sighed. "I meant being here without Eleanor."

Emily rubbed my shoulder. "That's how I feel every day when I get up in the morning."

"I know." I wiped a set of tears away. "She caught us once. My mother. She was coming to pick me up from Rosewood. You and Thomas weren't there, and Eleanor and I were in the hot tub. Totally naked. I don't think my mother had seen my naked since she'd changed my diaper. I was so embarrassed. The whole ride home we were silent until we were almost home. She told me to never do it again and warned me that if I did, I should never let my father find out. We never talked about it again."

"I know. She told me."

"What?" I lifted my head.

"She thought I should 'be aware of what was going on in my house.' I told her I already was. She didn't like that answer."

"You were?"

"Didn't she ever tell you moms have eyes in the back of their heads?"

I laughed, and Emily kissed my head again.

"She didn't like what you and Eleanor were doing. She was very adamant about that. But she knew trying to stop it would only make it worse. And she knew you were safer in our house. That's why she didn't argue when I asked if you could move in."

"Asked?"

"Suggested."

"Threatened sounds more like it."

Emily pulled me closer. "Someone had to look after you."

I leaned up, kissing her cheek. "You've been more of a mother to me than she has."

She wrapped her arms around me, hugging me so hard I would have complained I couldn't breathe if I weren't so glad to be in her arms.

"Whatever you do," she managed as she squeezed the oxygen from my lungs, "Don't die before I do."

It didn't take me long to mourn. I had just permitted myself to power through and finish the portrait when January 6 arrived, so I shut off faster than I'd turned on as I watched my country's capitol collapse at the hands of lunatics.

Sissy spent the day crying. Her hormones had caused a meltdown the day before because she shrunk a pair of socks she never wore in the dryer, so this was like the world was ending, and the longer we watched, the harder it was for me to not break down with her. Friends from Europe texted and asked if I was alright and what I thought, which annoyed me since I didn't live anywhere near the capital.

If they thought my opinion was anything except raw, gut-wrenching disgust, they didn't know me.

Emily tried to turn the news off and encourage us to do something else, but not knowing what was happening only upset Sissy more. I didn't want to leave her side, so Emily left us alone while she returned to goat feeding or whatever farming task was occupying her that day.

One day after she was gone, these tasks might occupy me, I thought as I watched her come and go, sweaty and sunburnt, to replenish her iced tea.

When the doorbell rang, I was glad for the distraction, and even though I didn't want to admit it, I was happy to see my sister.

We didn't hug, and Sissy looked at her skeptically while I introduced them as though asking with her eyes if this was really my sister.

We'd looked alike once before she'd had children, and I hadn't had any clothes except my school uniform and her hand-me-down dresses. Her hair was cut in the usual mom style, and the color had faded from blonde to light brown. Then there was the age difference, and between the six days since I'd seen her and this one, she appeared to have aged an extra year.

"Congratulations," my sister said, nodding to Sissy's stomach, "I'm glad you're keeping the baby."

"Technically Kitty is," Sissy responded, and before the topics became political or personal, added, "I'm sorry about your mother."

"Thank you," my sister said in a way that showed she meant it, "I heard about your father. I'm sorry."

"Thank you." Sissy hardly meant it.

After a period of awkward standing around, Sissy turned off the TV, saying she wanted to lie down. As she left, she and I kissed, her hands rubbing up and down my arms so they still felt warm once she was gone, making me blush as my sister and I sat.

"You know it doesn't bother me that you like girls. Well, at least I try not to let it go. I don't think you're going to hell for it or anything like that."

I couldn't help but laugh. I knew she meant well, but when I pictured the reactions my friends back in Vienna would have, it seemed ridiculous. "Did Mom?" I asked, and as soon as I did, I regretted that, too, in case the answer was yes.

"No, she didn't," my sister said, pulling a binder from her bag. "I found this in Mom's things and thought you should have it."

Our mother was an obsessive scrapbooker. Every birthday, sporting event, and church festivity was carefully documented, captioned, and pressed into a binder that sat on the shelf in anticipation of being shown off to company that hardly ever came.

When I opened this one, I saw instantly that it had never been shown to visitors.

There was none of the usual commentary my mother wrote in the margins, but it was the best record of my career that I'd found, probably because there were no words to distract from the photographs and photos of paintings. A few interviews were scattered about, and as I leafed through the pages, my sister said there were copies of every magazine I'd edited hidden in her things.

"I'm guessing she left out the sex tape," I joked, which made my sister laugh.

"I wish you'd seen their faces when they saw the news about that. There was a sermon on sexual morality the Sunday after it came out. You were even named. Multiple times."

My hand tensed at the corner of a page featuring an image from before Eleanor's death. From the painting pictured, one never would have guessed that my other pieces were so dark. "Yet you and Mom still went to that church every Sunday."

"We couldn't just quit."

"Why not? I did."

"Yeah, but you're-"

"A lesbian?"

She sighed. "That's not how faith works, Katherine."

"No, but it is how church works."

I'd been to a church for Danny Evergreen's funeral, but aside from that, I couldn't remember the last time I'd stepped foot in one, not even as a tourist.

Every single Sunday went by without me missing it.

"I'm not you," she said with such certainty it startled me. "I can't not live the way I was raised. Church might have been miserable for you, and that breaks my heart, but it was the world for me when I was a kid. It still is. I can't approve of the way you live your life, but that doesn't mean I hate you for it."

Her words touched me, but they didn't erase years of misery, especially when I thought they should have been there years ago when I was locked in the chicken coop, when our siblings had teased me, and when Eleanor had died.

"After Eleanor died," my sister admitted. "Mom nearly left. She was worried. She said she'd never forgive herself if something happened to you."

"You mean if I killed myself?"

"Yes."

I closed the binder, trying not to picture my mother standing up to my father. "Why did she stay?" I asked.

"You know why."

I wasn't the only one my father had hit.

The back door slid open, and Emily's voice sounded bright as she said it was good we'd stopped watching the news. Then she saw us, and her pitch faltered.

"Oh. Mary. It's nice to see you. Are you staying for dinner?"

My sister shook her head as she stood, saying she best be getting back.

"Didn't you have a baby?" Emily asked.

"Yes. A boy. Andy. Katherine met him."

"Congratulations! I'm sorry. We should have sent a gift. Kitty, why didn't you tell me?"

I shrugged.

"Katherine's always been the quiet one," my sister noted.

Emily laughed as we went to the door. "Yes, she has. Well, it'll be nice for the baby to have a cousin to play with."

My sister and I laughed, waving instead of hugging goodbye. When the door was shut, I glared at Emily.

"What?" Emily insisted. "She's your sister. Why shouldn't your kids play together?"

I went back to the living room to grab the binder before bouncing up the stairs.

"I'm an only child! If I had a sister, I'd want our children to play together even if we didn't get along."

"Our relationship is complicated."

"All relationships are!"

"Not my relationship with art, which is why I'm going to go paint."

CHAPTER TWENTY-SEVEN

M y skin cried for my mother's touch. I neither anticipated nor wanted this burning, but as the days ticked by, I began to thaw. Sissy's growing stomach reminded me that once I had been as small as the baby inside her, dependent on my mother's body for nourishment so basic that without the safety of her cells, I wouldn't have been able to survive.

Back then, I hadn't been a lesbian or sinner in her eyes, not even boy or girl, but wholly hers in a time during which she loved me most, before I became a child besides the demure Christ-like one she wanted.

During this period of mourning, it was tempting to return to being tiny, to let Emily coddle me so I could continue the fantasy that her womb was the one out of which I had crawled.

Yet I knew if I did that, I would never grow up, and when there was a beating heart that would shift from needing Sissy to needing me, I had to become a woman, so when I wasn't immersed in my fantastical world of paint, I gave myself to baby preparations.

Eleanor's old room was being converted into a nursery, and within the first weeks of the new year, it wasn't recognizable. Its bright pink walls had been painted pale purple to match the trim of the light yellow curtains.

It was still hard to find manual labor because of the pandemic, so Emily put her cowboy fucks to work, and what they couldn't do, she and I did ourselves. She suggested I paint some sort of mural. When I said

I'd rather wait until we knew the gender, Emily pointed out that I was always the one advocating gender neutrality.

"Besides, Sissy told me she doesn't want to know until the birth."

"What?" I exclaimed as I looked up from the color palettes. "But I want to know!"

"Well, you can have the doctor tell you but not Sissy."

"But if I know it's a girl and paint pink unicorns, Sissy will know."

"I never expected you to want to paint pink unicorns."

The power of cultured gender norms was pervasive. In the past months, I'd daydreamed of ballet classes and dolls despite never having enjoyed either.

I retaliated against this realization and painted the most gender-neutral scene I could think of. I had just finished when news of a cold front captured the headlines. The closer it came and the colder it became, the more we began to realize it was real.

Luckily, Rosewood was literally ready for nuclear fallout.

"Thomas's parents were paranoid during the Cold War," Emily explained as she showed us a cellar stacked with canned goods, water bottles, and ammunition. She gave the statistics on how many people could survive for how long, adding that she came once a year to check the expiration dates as she pointed to a chart hanging on the wall with numbers and instructions. "We have our own generator and there's enough meat and vegetables in the freezers, so we'll be fine."

"How did I never know this existed?" I asked as I picked up a can of baby food and wondered why Emily had replenished the shelf two years ago when no babies lived here.

"There's a lot about Rosewood that you don't know."

And as the roads froze and it became impossible for Emily's cowboy fucks to make the drive, she asked if I wouldn't mind helping out with their tasks, making me realize that statement was more accurate than I'd imagined possible.

Ranching was not work.

It was labor.

Long, laborious loving of land and longing for the sun to set so I could return to my lover's arms reassured that I had done all I could to keep her safe from the cold, too weary to making love and loving not making it and merely lying in her arms and wishing morning would never come yet comforted that it would, because if the sun did not rise as it was so ordained, there seemed no purpose to this monotonous life.

Rosewood would exist beyond my years as it had ages before. My child would tend its sheep and yield its crops, and if it froze again, that child would cover its pipes and plants as I taught it, learning as I went along as Emily did.

This cold was new for her, for the state, and for everyone in it.

Not even in London or Vienna, where the winters had been harsh, had there been such snowfall that a white shroud was cast over the land.

Sissy remained inside, where she was lucky to stay warm, whereas Emily froze with me in the fields. She was stronger than me and more accustomed to this work, but her body carried twenty-five more years than mine. She exhausted easily, retreating to the comforts of a home with warm tea as often as she could, leaving me alone in what felt like a winter without end.

Far from the house, though still in sight, I feared falling and freezing into the ice, forgotten until a new age thawed the thick permafrost only for my body to be found from a future in which Rosewood's walls had fallen and Sissy and Emily, and I were lost to history without me having known my child or finished my painting.

My heart pounded, blood pumping hot against the layers of fat and epidermis struggling against the cold.

I was by the barn. Its wood was frozen solid, and the color that had looked dull a week ago in the sunshine came to life against the dead white winter and echoes of Eleanor.

Blood beat through my eyes, my irises seeing her red over the snow, laughing despite the stiffness of her corpse, her voice carrying over the silent snow so that in this second. It could have been several, maybe even a minute or two or many as time stretched across the solid horizon and streamlined sky. I was sure death and Eleanor awaited.

Only death did not come, and I did not die, returning without realizing to Rosewood as my feet trudged through the trenches of slush.

In such an uncertain time, I had no energy or resources to waste on paint, so I could not escape to my studio to face the reality I had seen with my imagination.

Still, every evening, art served its escape as Sissy read words I'd once heard and somewhat forgotten, poetry or stories or stories in poetry, it didn't matter which so long as they were more beautiful than the world outside.

When she was tired of reading, we listened to Emily's records, lying on the couch with our eyes closed as we imagined living in that melody. After enough warm whiskey, I believed we were the notes waltzing up and down their octaves.

As soon as my head touched my pillow, the light of the world went out, and I was happily not but nearly dead.

On the day that the three-day winter vanished, I woke with certainty that I had not died at the barn or during the winter's worst days.

This cold clarity made me question whether any of it had been real or merely the workings of my mind, if I had feared for my life and seen Eleanor rotting and screaming in the snow or if I really had ever seen her and if for the past seven years, her hauntings had not been dreamed.

Beside me, Sissy stirred but still slept.

I rested a hand on her stomach, cherishing what I was certain was true.

Spring was coming, and I would be a mother.

CHAPTER TWENTY-EIGHT

In sync with Sissy's, the earth's skin expanded, grass sprouting from cracked clay and flowers struggling from soil to slant into extended sunshine as sunsets lingered, daylight lengthening, the portrait progressing.

When the last edition of the magazine was submitted, my dedication to motherhood increased, and my interest in painting anything but the portrait vanished.

I stocked up on diapers and ordered multiple copies of every book ever printed on parenting and baby psychology.

I joined Emily in her tasks around Rosewood, and the more I uncovered, the more I remembered memories I'd suppressed or lost since Eleanor's suicide.

It was tantalizing to think of those days through the filter of death and forget that though now I wept, here once I had laughed while wading through the creek to escape the heat, crouching down to cover our skin in what scarce coolness could be found amidst drought, splashing drops from the stream over each other's peeling skin, singing serenades and wringing water from uncombed and unkempt curls.

I incorporated these scenes into the portrait, adding color and brightness to spots previously covered with shadow. I reminisced with Emily while we worked, chatting with her late into the night while Sissy slept.

One evening, as I emerged from recollections, I checked my phone.

Texts from Lana Lane were not out of the ordinary. We checked in on each other occasionally, and that evening, we began to chat as we often had.

She was coming to Texas soon and had heard I'd moved back, so she wanted to see me. Naturally, I wanted to see her, and with our flirty texts, I was taken back to late-night laughs in London and sleepless siestas in Spain. Had Sissy not been there to remind me I wasn't in either of those places, I could have texted Lana all night.

Sissy's sexual desire had diminished. She was tired, too tired even to let me make love to her. As I lay nearly alone in the darkness with Lana's texts still fresh in my mind, I recalled how I'd let Lana love me, how we'd lain awake so long we hardly slept.

Sissy didn't love me like that.

I never let her, but Lana had never let me stop her.

The later we came into spring, the more we texted, and my screen became a retreat from ranching and preparing for mothering.

With every ding from the device, my face brightened. In the early days, this was easy to hide. Still, before long, Emily and Sissy began to ask what or who divided my attention, and the first few times, I made excuses. Still, when they saw the name Lana Lane flash across the screen, there wasn't much to do except tell the truth.

Sissy didn't seem angry, but that didn't mean she was pleased. When I asked if she was upset or wanted to talk about it, she said she was tired and wanted to sleep. The next day, I overheard her sobbing to Emily, but as soon as I came in the room, she silenced her cries and excused her tears as pregnancy hormones.

I didn't press her and continued to text Lana, chatting about any and every topic, her children, my coming child, my art, her movies, everything except our past.

In an abundance of adrenaline and eagerness, I invited her to Easter.

She accepted within seconds.

I cursed the ease of communication and dreaded the moment I'd broach the subject with my lover and hostess.

Since learning Rosewood would one day be mine, I moved with more certainty about the house, but it was still not mine in deed or mind, and there were times I couldn't help but think of myself as Emily's guest.

I chose a moment when they were both relaxed. It was dinner on a Saturday. Nothing tied our schedules to weekdays and ends, but we abided by the Christian sensibility that Sunday was for resting and that Saturday evening was the most relaxing section of our seven-day cycles.

Emily had already consumed enough wine that she was smiling at every second word we said, so when I first mentioned Lana, she seemed almost glad. I talked a bit about an upcoming film shoot in the area, easing into issues about scheduling, holidays, and being separated from her family, breezing over my invitation as though I'd already mentioned it.

Sissy's face flushed as Emily sipped a gulp of wine.

I attempted to fill the silence with excuses, but Emily waved them aside. "It doesn't bother me so long as Sissy doesn't mind."

"I don't care," said Sissy so quickly it was clear the answer was rushed, and I added that she could change her mind. She nodded but said she wouldn't, and the conversation shifted by necessity away from the subject before naturally circling back to it.

"Do you see Lana often?" Sissy asked.

I shrugged, saying every so often, avoiding Emily's gaze. She knew the last two times I'd seen Lana, I'd slept with her.

"How did the two of you meet?" Sissy persisted.

"A Twelfth Night party."

"A what?"

"It was a costume party on the twelfth day of Christmas. In Soho. In London. I was doing my residency. It was a crazy mix of lesbians and drag queens, all artists or artist wannabees. Lana wasn't the only famous actress, but she was the most famous, though she would have stood out even if she wasn't. She was wearing this over-sexed cowgirl outfit with glittery make-up. She had some challenge from a drinking game in which she had to kiss the first person she saw, and that was me."

"What were you dressed up as?"

"A very unsexy cowgirl."

I said a bit more about our relationship, skimming over the sensation of my first kiss with Lana, of falling for her before I'd seen her face, dreaming of what she might look like while her lips were still wet on mine, gasping for air as she shoved her tongue in my throat and grasped to catch it back as she pulled away. I saw who she was and felt my heart stop and then sore again when she took my hand and sat me down beside her, claiming me for that night and many that followed.

I couldn't tell Sissy that, compared with our first sex, Lana's and mine had been chaotic bliss, a ripping of clothes from the second my apartment door shut us into solitude, that she had me meet her family within a week, that she took me to my first strip club, swept me off my easel to a spontaneous trip to the country where she absorbed my body and soul into hers, on screen in the sensual video we made and off it in the sheets.

In her state, Sissy couldn't handle that.

So in the days that preceded Lana's coming, I slipped more and more into my studio, blending the paints intended for Eleanor's portrait with the image of myself as I relived memories that, as I smeared lines into a smile and suppressed shapes and colors into a character I could only comprehend through creation, were the happiest of my adult life, for with Lana, I'd been utterly and entirely free to be myself, to breathe, and as I inhaled fresh paint and smelled it sticking to the canvas, I recalled the sex without the tape, her kisses during our first viewing in which we declared I'd created art.

Not a work of art.

Art.

As soon as the word passed from lips still soaked from sucking mine, she exclaimed she should take me to Spain.

As I closed my eyes, paint clinging to my cheeks, I saw pieces I hadn't seen in seven years but still remembered in riveting detail. I sensed the resurgence of a soul whose colors had faded. Set to sleep by scandal and suicide, she stirred from slumber, and was restored.

CHAPTER TWENTY-NINE

M y soul restored itself to Spain, to Madrid, where it truly and completely lost itself in Lana Lane, who, in the course of a single visit to an art museum, re-invented herself more times than any actress I'd ever seen, except none of it was an act.

The Lana who observed the psychologically disturbed paintings from one century was not Lana who stood before pastel landscapes from the next nor Lana weeping at the black paintings of one artist as Lana smiling at the summer scenes from the same hand.

Between three floors and thousands of years of art, more Lana Lanes than would ever appear on screen revealed themselves to me.

Stiff-faced and stony-eyed underneath the subtle 60s headscarf and oversized but nondescript specs, she was an average admirer of art, not a sensual movie star in disguise. When I looked in the mirror with her next to me, I was not an aspiring and moderately successful artist. I was not American, not Texan, and she was not; we were not, but we were, and in the tremor of her hand, the loss of air in her gasp as her lips separated in admiration for art, she was to me all and none of what she was to ordinary people, no what, but the epitome of who, and when she sipped her final drops of red wine, lifting her eyebrows as she stole the last tapas, and when she dropped her dress and made love over freshly-pressed hotel sheets, Lana Lane was the epitome of her, of she, of living, breathing, being.

The weekend lasted less than seventy-two hours, but each turn of the long clock had lasted more than a lifetime of lives.

When it was over, and now long after the last drips of wine have worn through my stomach and the flush from the Spanish sun has faded from my cheeks, memories of Madrid manifest so magnanimously I muse over whether those who's who'd stood before paintings and palaces were people or Lana Lane and Kitty Kunz, whether it was Kitty Kunz who made love to Lana Lane or whether Lana made love to a whom, one woman of many, a face as interchangeable as any *mujer* or *femme* on display in a museum.

This was the sort of musing Eleanor no left no room for.

She appeared in London, unannounced and uninvited, the day Lana and I returned from our weekend getaway.

Surprise, she said, a coy smile sliding upwards as I shoved my over-sized suitcase through my apartment's undersized entrance.

In twenty-four years, Eleanor had never surprised me with so much as a slice of birthday cake.

She knew about Lana and the sex tape we'd made a few weeks prior, but I didn't know she knew.

I played along, nervously smiling, as I showed pictures from my trip specially selected to exclude Lana.

I should have known something was wrong when, before we even kissed, she suggested we go to Spain, where I'd told her I'd been alone, but she obviously knew I hadn't.

Next week, she insisted.

It was Easter, and she was already in Europe, so why not?

So, within three days of returning, I booked another plane to Madrid.

When with Lana, meandering through museum after museum, my mind had flowed from one woman to another. There was Lana, a multitude of women in whose eyes' meaning was lost, and suddenly, there was Eleanor. Then Lana would laugh, and there was Lana again.

When I'd told Lana of Eleanor, she pecked my cheek without a word or jealousy.

With Eleanor, there was only room for Eleanor.

Women in paintings drove her into envy. Glances at girls in cafes sent her eyes darting in all directions.

Eleanor disliked Spanish food, despised Spanish wine, detested Spanish time. Late dinners stressed her stomach. Sunshine scorched her skin. A change from the big city could suit her.

Granada, she suggested, a city that was a slate without memories of my other lover.

Except Granada was not empty.

As the sun beat and browned my skin, spices subdued my sense of space while we wandered through tightly squeezed streets in search of nourishment during the *Semana Santa*, during which the Holy Week procession of the dead god and mourning mother passed and stained the air with incense. When we found food, the wine circumvented my stomach, shooting straight to a dehydrated mind that slurred through dinner and stumbled into supper, shifting from poetic expressions of affection to affective exclamations of the Alhambra as it appeared through glimpses caught between ceramic ceilings and half-closed curtains.

Sometime, for in Spain, there was always time that was imprecisely some, she persuaded me to bed, but as she seized my body, my mind betrayed her in our kisses as, under my eyelids, I saw Lana.

I overslept.

The sheets were cold, but when Eleanor returned with coffee in hand, her smile shone brighter than the Saturday sun. She kissed me, caressed me with salts she'd bought from the hammam, showered me with sex. Sensuality subdued me, so not until her skin was crumpling in cold soil did I understand the veils of smoke and spice that strung Saturday into Sunday were distractions.

Despite the Easter celebrations, we'd seen the Alhambra, against whose backdrop we sipped sangria past sunset and stumbled down cobblestones to our overpriced hotel into priceless silk sheets and sex that settled into my skin through sleep, the orgasms still fresh as we strolled through the streets the next day behind the procession of the risen god, sneaking away hand-in-hand to a tourist trap of a tea shop.

It was an odd time of day and nearly empty, and the Muslims, ambivalent to the Christian procession, were watching the news. I ordered a hookah and tea and cuddled into the couch, nuzzling my head into Eleanor's embrace and ignoring the uneasiness of the veiled woman preparing the hookah as her eyes averted from our unabashed affection.

When she left, I waited for Eleanor to criticize that smoking wasn't healthy or that the tea was too hot.

Instead, she kissed me.

And kissed me.

And sometime and somewhere, between kisses or after smokes, Lana spoke.

To push her voice from my head, I kissed Eleanor harder, but the voice grew with a dub of standard Spanish. The harder I kissed, the louder and clearer the voices cut through the layers of smoke.

Amidst the foreign sounds and her voice, I understood.

Lana Lane. Sex tape.

My mouth dried up.

Kitty Kunz. *Artista americana. Vive en London.*

Eleanor bit my frozen lip.

"Eleanor," I gasped, pulling away as she smothered my lips. I thought she hadn't heard, but when I looked into her eyes, the spices from the tea soured and the sweetness of the hookah became bitter. Her grin unmasked its smirk. "You've ruined us."

Us? She sliced me with her voice. Since when had there been another *us* aside from her and me?

She wept; I cried.

We left Granada without another glimpse of the Alhambra and, with hardly another word, she for the New World and I to the Old, except the city to which I went seemed like another world entirely as cameras flashed at the airport and outside the gates of Lana's house.

Phones rang nonstop, and she and her husband shouted until he cracked and checked himself into a rehab center, dropping divorce papers and leaving crying children with them.

The only call I answered was Emily's.

Emily demanded no explanation. She loved me, no matter what happened between Eleanor and me. I was always welcome home. I thanked her. I loved her, too.

Eleanor wouldn't answer, and if she had, I don't know what I would have said except I still loved her.

Loving Lana couldn't make me stop loving Eleanor. Lana understood, but Eleanor didn't, and loving Lana had shown me that Eleanor could not covet me.

"I'm coming out," Lana confessed as she stroked my hair in bed.

Since the whole world had seen our sex, we weren't having any, but we still held each other. "Of the house?" I asked but quickly realized what she meant.

She sighed as her fingers released my split ends. "Sometimes I wonder if you're actually a lesbian or just ... I don't know. Lost in your own world."

I wasn't sure what she meant, but I let her go on.

"I'll do it on television," she explained, "I already have enough calls from talk shows."

Millions had watched our private sex, and now those same viewers demanded a public apology for something they never should have seen.

"I don't want you to do anything you don't want to, but if you want to come with me, you can."

I didn't. It wasn't the world's business whom I slept with, and even if it were, I wouldn't make Eleanor watch me declare love for another woman. She might have been the one to show me naked to the world, but she shouldn't have stumbled across the tape and seen me loving another woman the way she'd wanted to be loved.

"Will you stay with me?" Lana asked.

"I'm already here."

She laughed, turning my face towards hers. Her hands were steady, but her voice shook, and as tears dropped, I came to know Lana Lane, the girl who had never been the Lana she wanted to be, the little Lana who wanted only to be loved.

"Not just for tonight. For good."

I couldn't go back to Eleanor, and without her, I wouldn't return to Rosewood or Texas or any other part of America.

So, I remained.

Lana's home was a doll house compared with Rosewood, but for the few weeks between Easter and May 12, it was our doll house.

We sowed spring soil and planted seeds. I painted several of my best pieces. We had sex without prohibiting our most innate desires.

Her children ran carelessly through the garden, and once the paparazzi found another story, we were left alone.

The coming out confession on the talk show was well-received.

Lana was a victim of an oppressive society. She and her husband had always been free to see other people. Hollywood shallowly self-acknowledged itself as the problem and patted itself on the back for its confession.

My name came up a few times in the news but was overshadowed by Lana's.

When Emily visited England to check on me, I asked about Eleanor. The sideways glance in her eyes answered more than Emily's words.

"She doesn't know I've come to see you. She doesn't talk to me much. Not since the divorce. She doesn't talk to Thomas, either. She says she's busy with law school, which is true. Probably. But I haven't seen her since y'all left Spain."

I glanced at Lana playing with her girls in the garden. "You're upset I chose Lana."

"All I want is for both of you to be happy," she sighed, "but you're Eleanor and Kitty. I can't think of one of you without the other."

"Eleanor isn't easy."

"I know," she brought her tea to her lips, "Trust me. I know."

It started to sprinkle, so Lana and her girls came in. Three children shouted over each other as they ran past me, the youngest asking if I'd help with a watercolor.

"Angela, Kitty has a guest," Lana said, picking the girl up. "Mrs. Pontell flew all the way from Texas to see her. It would be rude for Kitty to ignore her."

The girl pouted, and I leaned over to kiss her cheek. "I'll read you an extra painting at bedtime."

She grinned at the compromise and stuck her thumb in her mouth. Lana pulled it out, rolling her eyes as she leaned in for a quick kiss with me, but it turned into a long one, a clock-stopping kiss that only a screaming child could interrupt.

When they left Emily and me alone, Emily asked what I meant by reading a painting.

"Just something I do for the girls. Why are you looking at me like that?"

She laughed, shaking her head. "It's just ... you and Eleanor never kissed in front of me."

Nor would we ever.

It was not long after that when Lana intruded into my studio, her face was so pale that I knew not to be angry about the interruption. She handed me a cell phone with Emily on the other line.

And I heard her tell me in broken words through a crummy speaker that Eleanor was dead.

CHAPTER THIRTY

F inality is the frightening thing in death. Every other ending contains possibilities, sequels, alternatives, or something, but in death, there is only decay.

The promise of Christianity was not mere incarnation or afterlife but the literal resurrection of the body, of flesh, of its blood.

Except for fornicators and suicides, there was no resurrection, reanimation of the heart, no resurgence of veined liquid, only centuries of sarcastic suffering, gnashing of teeth, and torturous tearing.

I did not believe it, but I'd been indoctrinated.

When Easter Sunday and Lana arrived, the portrait was still unfinished.

On Friday and Saturday, I'd sat a slave to it, painting until my eyes struggled to stay open, beginning to feel this task was my punishment, not my purgatory.

Near noon on Sunday, Emily knocked. Despite me not answering, she entered, drawing the curtains and propping the windows open.

A brush had fallen by my sleepy head. She picked it up, rubbing the stain on the floor as I reached for my eyes. She pulled my hands away before they could touch my eyelashes, explaining, "Your fingers are dirty."

I lifted my shirt, but it wasn't any cleaner.

Emily sighed, wiping my sleepy crows with her fingers. "You look so little when you sleep. It makes me miss our Easter egg hunts."

"Next year you can hide Easter eggs."

"You can hide Easter eggs." She wiggled my earlobe but didn't waste time reminiscing, reminding me that Lana would be there soon.

I sat up, looking at the portrait.

Emily glanced over her shoulder. "You need a break," she sighed.

Though dissatisfied, I obeyed.

In the shower, colors bled from my skin, staining the drain until I rubbed myself slippery and shed chunks of clear conditioner with my tangly hair.

For two days, I'd been lost in memories of my happiest days, painting without looking, seeing not the marks of my hands but the makings of my mind until I looked in the mirror and saw escapism's toll and smeared my face with Sissy's moisturizer, slathering my underarms in plain deodorant. If scents hadn't sickened Sissy's sensitive stomach, I would have hidden under spiced perfume.

As I was dressing, the door creaked open.

Seeing Sissy sent the dreams of the past two days to the distance, but before I had the chance to speak, she said, "Lana Lane's here."

"Oh." My smile faltered. "You can just call her Lana, you know."

To me, Lana Lane wasn't Lana. The former meant fame and scandal, the latter love.

"Well, then, Lana's here," she said, adding, "She's beautiful."

"I know. I spent our whole relationship feeling self-conscious."

Sissy sat beside me, and the weight of her body pressing into the bed made me recognize the implications of my comment. Instead of apologizing for saying the truth, I leaned over for a kiss.

She returned it, but not sincerely, so I rested my hands on her shoulders, pressing my forehead against hers. "What is it?"

I felt her sigh under my lips. "I've missed you."

Stroking the sides of her neck with my finger, I pushed my lips into hers. "I'm sorry."

"This isn't easy," she resisted.

I tugged my lips back, nodding a nod that shouldn't have been my only offering of understanding. "I know. If I'm not done when the baby comes, I'll stop. I promise."

She nodded, then laughed as her eyes darted to my dress. "Are you really wearing black on Easter?"

"Oh," I glanced down and saw the color for the first time, "No. I'll change."

A first glimpse of Lana was overwhelming for anyone.

First came the stun, that sharp piercing of incapacitating beauty. Then came the fluttering, stammering, and fame.

For some, fame never faded, and they stood starstruck and stumbling over compliments. For others, disillusion settled. For me, the past flashed through my nerves, coursing back in chemicals of satisfaction soured by lost chances.

Kisses on the cheek sent me back to the citrus scents of Spain, the drumming of her fingers on my back to filming the tape in her home in England. The flash of her smile reflected in mine, and I remembered her daughters' laughter when they wiggled loose teeth or hid behind their hands to play peek-a-boo. The oldest two had double-digits by now. One was a teenager. Lana was forty-five. Her skin had creased, her flaming hair faded to soft strawberry.

Yet her spark still shone, and long-term fame had implanted a shimmer that made even Emily seem ordinary as Rosewood appeared a hollow set where any second the sunset would fade into greenscreen or someone would shout cut to shut off the cameras, and that in an instant Lana Lane could dissolve into pixels, step out of costume, and shed her make-up.

"It seems bigger than I remember," Lana said as we showed her the home.

"I re-decorated," Emily explained. "It wouldn't work for a Western set anymore."

"It never would have," Lana noted, "It's too real for the movies." She'd said that when she'd come before, but it still sounded novel from her lips.

Sissy asked what they meant, and Lana leaped into the saga of filming her famous Western, which Sissy had somehow never seen. My lovers lost themselves in conversation as I helped Emily prepare our meal. Sissy was still in the starstruck phase, and Emily was in disillusioned apathy, reminding me of Eleanor's general state of disillusionment.

Throughout the day, Emily muttered micro-aggressions against veganism, Lana's diet of the moment, supposedly for environmental reasons. Anyone who drove a car like hers couldn't intelligently care about the environment, hissed Emily as she tried to hide that she was upset I'd invited Lana. The coldness reached iciness at the dinner table when she asked if Lana's girls didn't miss her when she was away so much.

Lana conceded that they did, dishing salad and shifting the conversation away from the accusation without acknowledging that's what it was by asking Sissy about her pregnancy.

Even while discussing the grotesque, Lana was charming, laughing off tales of vomiting and grinning at the mention of diarrhea.

By the end of the meal, even Emily was endeared, and her cold reserve had softened to quiet disinterest.

"So, Kitty, what are you working on?" Lana asked as I helped clean the dishes. Lana had offered help, but Emily wouldn't let her.

Sissy, whose energy faded faster than a tired toddler, had excused herself to lie down.

Before answering, I glanced at Emily as though needing permission. Eye contact was avoided, so I answered that I was painting a portrait of Eleanor.

Lana adjusted her hair.

The dishwasher hummed as it started, so Emily had to speak up to be heard. "Lana, would you like some coffee or tea?"

"Tea would be wonderful."

"Kitty?"

I nodded. The kettle clicked.

We'd already asked about Lana's work. She was filming a long-awaited sequel to the great Western she'd starred in at the beginning of her career. We'd discussed the films she'd made since we'd broken up and complained about how she'd been pigeonholed into lesbian films and sidekick roles. She'd glossed over her relationships, confining our conversation to small talk.

Now that Sissy was gone, our stiffness loosened.

The relief that the adults were now free to speak sent my heart beat-skipping as I realized that wasn't a sensation I should have felt when my girlfriend left the room, especially if we were to be parents together.

As the kettle rose to a boil, Emily pulled out two mugs. "I'm rather tired, too. I think I might head to bed early. Lana, you're welcome to stay the night. Kitty can show you a guest room."

"Thank you, but I'll probably drive back soon."

"Whatever you want." Emily handed us our mugs. Before leaving, she gave me a good night hug and kiss, squeezing me tight so she could whisper, "Make good choices."

I rolled my eyes as she walked away, and though she couldn't have heard, Lana laughed once Emily was gone, giving a sympathetic look.

The last time Lana and I had seen each other and had sex had ended one of Lana's relationships and escalated into another short-lived scandal.

"I'm sorry about your mother," Lana offered.

I smiled but didn't thank her even though I knew she meant it.

"Sissy's sweet."

"Sweet?" It wasn't the adjective I'd wanted.

"Yeah. I see why you like her. She's artsy. You're an artist."

"Artsy? She's an artist, too."

"Right. Sorry. I forgot how picky you are about words."

"You should be, too. You're an artist."

She made a sound similar to a laugh as she sipped her tea. It was a sound I'd heard when we'd been together: suppressed yet unconcealable self-doubt, except the severity of her self-consciousness increased with age.

"I'm an actress. Acting is an art," she conceded.

"But?"

The sound came again. "But I feel more like I'm acting off-screen than on."

"Everyone is always acting."

"I know. All the world's a stage."

Lana complained about the most over-quoted line in acting more than me, and her recitation sounded like submission.

"I just feel like no one takes me seriously as an actress since the sex tape, or since Eleanor died."

My neck tensed sharply. She said the name so effortlessly.

"Every script I read is for a lesbian or some woman who's so over-sexed it's like they're making fun of the fact that I'm a lesbian. None are real roles. They're just lines they want to read from a hot body. And I take them. Then I hate myself for taking them. And I hate myself for taking this stupid sequel that's basically no better than fan-fiction of my early career."

"You've encouraged lots of girls to come out."

"And all the copycat suicides after Eleanor?"

Even had I and, therefore, Lana and thereby the sex tape not been associated with Eleanor's suicide, the method, location, and wealth would have made it newsworthy.

The therapist in grief counseling said copycats were to be expected, like there was nothing ordinary about a young woman leaping on top of a bull to her death.

Lana and I attended therapy together, but I stopped going altogether when I left her. I made my affairs my excuse for leaving, but Lana had always known about them and never cared.

At that moment, I found myself supporting Lana with sympathy I never afforded myself.

"She posted the sex tape," I reminded Lana, "I think she had it planned the second she saw it, maybe even before. I wouldn't be surprised if she had planned it all out before we went to Spain."

"Does Emily know Eleanor was the one who posted it?"

I shrugged and sipped my tea.

"You've never mentioned it?"

"We don't talk about her."

"Right. Her." Lana's eyes widened as she brought her tea to her mouth. "After seven years you still can't say her name."

"Eleanor," I said, flatly, coldly, letters strung together in a particular order without constituting a name.

Lana made another one of those sounds that was distinctly hers that she made to express words she couldn't quite say, this one just as self-conscious as the last but with more mockery.

I chose silence.

"Would you show me the portrait?"

"No. It's for Emily."

"Right. I understand."

"But I did a self-portrait I'll show you."

We tip-toed up to the studio, where I made her wait at the door until I'd turned Eleanor's portrait around and retrieved mine. She squinted as I flicked on the lamp, but as her eyes adjusted to the art, they softened.

She stared for some time without saying anything, and as she was about to, I stopped her by powering on the computer.

"Sissy took some good photos of me."

But as I clicked on the folder, Sissy's bare, bruised body flashed on the screen.

"Oh!" Lana exclaimed before I could click out of them. "Don't tell me you did that to her."

"Why would you think that?"

"You sometimes like it rough."

Lana was the only person to whom I'd confessed Eleanor's violence. After Eleanor's death, Lana knew of my affairs instantly because of the bruises I'd sought out. Instead of becoming angry, she'd held ice packs on my body without asking. When she eventually confronted me, I thanked her by packing my bags.

The two times we'd seen each other since the break-up, both ending in sex, she'd spent half the night kissing freshly cut scars.

"Her ex-boyfriend did it," I explained.

"Is he the father?"

"Unfortunately."

"Did she report it?"

I shook my head. I was glad she didn't give me a speech. I knew we should have, but I wasn't going to take that decision away from Sissy.

Her fingers traced the veins of my shoulder, and, without meaning to, I rested my head back into her body as she began to massage my shoulders.

"She's beautiful," Lana sighed as I scrolled to photos without the bruises. "If you weren't sleeping with her, I would."

"Even now?"

"You mean even now that she's – what – seven months pregnant?"

"Yeah."

Lana's hands ran down the length of my arms as she bent behind me, propping her head over my shoulder and pointing to a picture she said was her favorite.

"Yeah, I would," she said again as though to prove it.

Emily's warning echoed through my mind, but so did Sissy's remarks earlier that Lana was beautiful.

"My husband and I were having sex when I went to labor for the first time."

"I didn't know you two ever had sex."

"How do you think I got pregnant?"

"You don't need sex to have a baby anymore."

"We did things the real way. And we would other times. Sometimes. Especially when I was pregnant. I guess having his child inside me turned him on."

"Is that even safe when you're so far along?"

"We would just have oral sex. Why? Haven't you two been doing it?" I shook my head. "Do you want to?"

I drew my head back, suddenly feeling how close Lana's face was to mine. "With you?"

The next sound she made was also like a laugh, except it was all confidence and affection as her face shifted to flirtatious.

"The three of us?" she suggested.

In seconds, my heartbeat skyrocketed.

"Let me ask Sissy," I couldn't say more quickly.

Initially, Sissy was eager, but when Lana joined us, she recoiled shyly into herself.

Sensing Sissy's self-consciousness, Lana eased into sex, starting by saying how beautiful she was, reassuring her with soft touches and sugary caresses.

She instructed me to hold Sissy, orchestrating our love with such experienced direction that Sissy came so strongly it seemed staged, and even though I was holding her, I couldn't help but believe it wasn't real. She'd been helpless in my arms before, but not so helpless her body fell limp as Lana continued to kiss her, caressing the stretching and swelling of her body as she worked her way up to Sissy's lips, stroking the edges of her face, holding Sissy's lips with her tongue before laying Sissy's head in my lap and lifting her own to mine. Her tongue brushed over my chapped lips, and sensing her desperation, I held out my arms. I let her fall into my embrace, allowing me to feel the pounding of her heart and shallowness of breath.

Her performance had seemed so effortless.

Melted in my arms, I understood the exhaustion of Lana's art, its synthesis of satisfaction of success and displeasure with the reality that her body hadn't been the one to feel the strength it inspired in another.

If all the world were a stage, and all of us actresses merely in it, then our bodies were simulations from a screen.

Embracing her bare skin, I thought I didn't care if this were reality or fiction, science or fantasy, if her body were hers or Sissy's, Eleanor's or mine, if we were dead or alive.

When I made love to her, fucking her on the floor and then the shower with Sissy sleeping in the background, I gave her what I'd always dreamed of giving, what every woman had accused me of withholding.

I shoved her onto the tiles, straddled and strangled her in slippery, soapy sweat, forcing her to ask me to stop, only to make her cry for more. Then, when she was bit and bruised and satisfied, I submitted my body to hers and released my soul into suffering.

And when we laid in bed late that night, Sissy and Lana asleep on either side, and I rested one hand on Lana's C-section scarred stomach and another on Sissy's and felt the finality of our scene falling over the curtain of Eleanor's control, I fell asleep with the certainty that this was not the end and anticipated, also, the rising of the sun.

CHAPTER THIRTY-ONE

The sun rose again that morning and the one that followed, and every morning that followed Lana's leaving, light unsewed my eyelids to show Sissy sleeping as soundly as a storybook character, revealing the illusion of my wet dreams that interchanged Lana with Eleanor and the reality of the life soon to come as, every day, Sissy's stomach inched upward and outward.

Lana returned to London or Los Angeles or some other exciting city for her next shoot. I couldn't keep track of where she lived. Still, wherever she'd ended up flying to, she texted frequently, sending photos of her girls, whom I hardly recognized with their added height and womanly features, reminding me that the crib wasn't complete, that we didn't have a car seat, and that the portrait wasn't finished and that I'd promised to stop painting if I wasn't done by the time the baby came, leading to more sleepless nights in my studio.

Since Lana left, the topic of sex hadn't been broached between Sissy and me, not even to reflect on the threesome during which we'd abandoned her.

The following day, she had seen the bruises on Lana's back and bite marks splotching my skin. And she knew that in the following days, I touched myself in the studio in front of Eleanor's incomplete image instead of making love to my living, breathing, heavily pregnant girlfriend whom I held in every other way without bringing myself to sex, my hand hardly hovering over her enlarged breasts, my lips only pecking hers. She seemed so delicate, more vulnerable than when her skin had been brown from her ex-boyfriend's bruises.

In the beginning of May, what should have been Sissy's graduation came and went.

The diploma arrived in the mail.

Sissy skipped the sad excuse for a virtual ceremony. We celebrated, setting aside our passive-aggressive conflicts and unaddressed issues so we could drink and dream them away for the span of a sunset.

After Emily and I emptied a bottle of bubbly, Emily pulled out her guitar and, around the fire pit, played songs I'd forgotten existed but remembered every line to as she struck the chords.

I didn't sing, only hummed along as Sissy sang in a voice deeper than the tones I'd heard muffled through her mask at the grocery store and more confident than the meek answers she'd given when she first showed me her work, stronger than the voice that had recited poetry by the beach.

I stopped humming and closed my eyes, leaning my head back and letting smoke fumes smother and subdue my senses as one song bridged to the next, cords crossing notes climbing in crescendo to a fall, and diminish, fading into silence itself a song of absences of itself since fire crackled and crickets chirped, coyotes howled, and horses neighed and a breeze bustled before Emily's fingers fidgeted over the frets to start a song simultaneously happy and sad, happy because it was easy to sing of sunshine amidst grey skies, and sad because it was misunderstood and because I could not recall the last time I'd heard Emily sing it or the last time I'd heard her sing at all, and because I'd heard her sing this song so many times and as soon as the initial string was struck, I saw Eleanor not as I imagined her, but through her mother's mind.

Emily started automatically as though this were the most natural song to play, going through the lyrics everyone knew, her voice softening as she sang, shifting to slow meditation of the less-known lines of melancholy until she could no longer form the words and hummed, encapsulating tone without committing to meaning.

When her pitch faltered, I opened my eyes.

The song was breaking her.

Of this song, Sissy had not sung a single note, had not even echoed the famous chorus that was so well-known it was impossible not to mouth the words. She could not know the story behind this song, not as it related to us, nor did she need to.

With her hands resting on her stomach and her eyes wet, Sissy shone with sympathy as she heard loss and reflected it, saw love, and felt it.

Anyone who heard Emily sing that song would understand the words, but I heard a private tongue for mother and daughter, the only love language of Emily's I did not speak, much less sing.

Her tone descended into tears.

Without a word, I scooted closer to her. As her nails ran down the strings to create a chord that sounded out of tune even though it wasn't, I pried her fingers from the frets, setting the guitar out of reach as Sissy left, silently, I suspect because she saw the inherent sanctity of me stilling my body as the strongest woman I knew shook, of her clutching my bones as though begging to never be released, convulsing and collapsing into my chest, shivering, wailing as Emily Pontell regressed not to the virgin of her maiden name, but a child, a baby, a life breathing and beating in the only arms that would hold it as I became mother, sister, daughter, and more than those titles meant, another breathing, beating life caring for another because there was no choice save to take this soul enclosed by skin and reassure it in its loneliness if only for the sake that the heart beating in my breast would believe it.

I brought her to her bed, tucked her under the covers as she had so often for me, brought my lips to her forehead and reassured her that the sun would come out tomorrow, and as I left, held the photograph of Eleanor to my heart, kissed it, and left it in the bed beside the sleeping mother, the song looping in my head on repeat, becoming louder and louder with Eleanor's giggles accompanying, laughing near maniacally as I opened my door and found the other breathing, heart-beating soul I loved awaiting in a tearless trance.

She'd prepared words, but not so certainly. Her speech was sincere, thought-out but unrefined and unrehearsed.

She did not want to be a mother, not now, not ever.

She had known this since the second she learned she was pregnant, but she had denied it so she could stay with me because she'd seen I did want the child, and all these thoughts culminated when she heard Emily sing that song.

If motherhood brought such sorrow, she wanted none of it.

The child would be mine. She would give it to me. She begged me to let her give me this baby.

It would not be so simple, I knew, but I wouldn't say.

Birth would change Sissy, transform me, tear us apart.

She worried about us as all young women worried about romance more than themselves, so I reassured her as a man might assuage a mistress with what she wanted to hear. But once she'd fallen asleep and I lay in bed and thought of the child, I knew this would not last forever. We would always love each other, but I would become to her what many older women had been to me: a lesson learned and love best left behind.

In the days that followed, I rose before the sun as though to soften the surprise Sissy felt waking in a future without me.

I finished the crib, and we formalized an adoption agreement.

Before the baby departed Sissy's body, it belonged to me, as before the portrait escaped my mind, it belonged to Emily.

The first days of May came and went. In the heat, Sissy gathered the flowers she could find from the fields of grayed grass, forming them into crowns to adorn our heads as we sat around the pool each night and pretended it was our summer instead of autumn.

As Eleanor's birthday approached, Emily and I withdrew into our-selves, Emily playing the piano at odd hours, times when she ordinarily would have been working around Rosewood, drinking more Cham-pagne and more expensive whiskey, letting two different cowboy fucks leave her room in the span of a single hour.

When the eve of Eleanor's day came, she was dry in soul as much as in skin and went to work as though the day were not extraordinary.

I ate my eggs and drank my coffee before Sissy woke, and when she was opening the door of our bedroom, I closed and locked my studio door.

CHAPTER THIRTY-TWO

I said or wrote – I cannot remember which – that skin yearns.

Screams or aches might follow, but words and letters are symbols, and I am an artist of truth, each creation containing elements thereof, every work except the portrait a piece as only Eleanor truly expresses its fullness, or so I believed as I poured paint and passion into a portrait promising to transfigure into her essence of art and life, of everything,

Thus, it came that this piece, this stretch of scratchy, torn canvas, came to contain skin.

Skin from my flesh that I pierced with a knife, draining my wrist for blood to be smeared, dizzying my mind as the liquid transfused my fluids with Eleanor's oils.

Before too much blood leaked, I wiped and wrapped my wrists, waiting for the wounds to heal while the canvas dried enough for me to move on since mere flesh was not enough.

In a perfect world, I would have broken bones and torn intestines, removed my still-beating heart, and wrapped them in canvas to create a sacrifice that matched the measures my soul had suffered for this woman who could never, neither through art nor memory, be met.

Not in life nor in death was any Eleanor except an image accessible: beauty, itself, encapsulated and forever frozen at twenty-five in a virgin who wasn't, whom only two people had known, one having given blood and body in birth, necessitating for this image only her thoughts, most of which had seeped into mine, but many of which I'd never heard and never would since I tore the pages from Emily's diary without reading them, careful at the seams not to rip the letters before dipping them in dark ink and admiring the darkness enveloping the page until the words ceased to exist and I threw the sopping scraps onto the canvas, careful that as the colors blended they didn't conceal the countenance they intended to reveal.

Throughout the process, Eleanor's face remained untouched, her eyes pristine as they gazed or glared while a gluey substance was smeared over the rest so it would retain its stick. As it dried, I gathered supplies, ignoring the encroaching of Eleanor's ghosts as, in the distance, I heard her criticize this corner or that color. I saw her peering from behind the curtain, smelled her spicy perfume sift through the sheets of air heavy with must, hiding the stench of paint and my own skin so that if I weren't engrossed in this task, my scent would have withered beneath hers right under my own nose.

I might have disappeared had her portrait not required my movement.

For years, it had been thus that I wandered without aim, waiting for purpose to present itself.

I gathered the tools and heaved the painting into my arms, staining my hands as I clasped its edges, struggling to manage the weight as I shuffled through the door and down the stairs, doubtlessly dripping drops of the portrait as I trenched through the fields of Rosewood, tall thickets tearing at my ankles until I reached the barn.

A rusty iron lock guarded the empty space. The wood broke against my weight, and I had to avoid splinters as I fell inside, cringing at the cockroaches that scattered as moonlight flooded the darkness. Something crunched underneath my step, and as I suppressed my disgust, I caught glimpse of a grin of bright teeth illuminated in the silhouette of a shade, a reminiscence of schadenfreude.

As I shivered, I dropped the canvas at my feet, catching bugs under its borders and bringing up dust as the frame thumped slightly off-center to the spot where the bull had been shot.

Before I began, I returned to the entrance to shed my clothes from their skin, dropping the fabric in the grass outside the barn.

Once bare, my hand lingered on the lock.

The door had been sealed when Eleanor died, or at least I had imagined it so. She would have closed it to have no escape.

It would have been right for me to do the same, to follow her steps and, as I closed my eyes, meet my end.

With pale moonlight saturating my squeezed eyelids, I saw her waiting, wanting me like I'd always wanted and how she never had, with open arms and parted lips prepared for my embrace in anticipation of our kiss, of the whispering of words I still awaited, for the touch I yet yearned, the flavors I'd forever sought.

I opened my eyes, and there were bugs.

They scattered from my feet, but some, oblivious to who or what I was, scuttled over and around my toes, settling so close that, had I not been so entranced, I would have screamed or cried and ran. In my state, I saw without sensing things from which, without reason, I didn't shy away from.

The act was mad; this portrait was cursed. Eleanor dead.

Her laughter was in my head, her grin in my mind and not before my eyes, her scents fixtures of fantasy.

The moon was nearly full and, through the rafters, forged shimmering light ripe for painting. Her eyes were bright but didn't blare, and mine worked softer than when they strained under the sun.

Still, they struggled to distinguish the tools I'd brought.

I knew I wasn't properly prepared; I wasn't Eleanor.

This was planned but not premeditated, not meticulously calculated and measured. I hadn't even stopped to think of last words for Sissy or Emily or ways to warn them should flames reach Rosewood, which, while I struck the match, occurred to me could happen.

The fluid was spread out, and I stepped back a second too late, except if it weren't for my panic, it might have been too soon.

My heart burst as the flicker sparked, froze as the flame ignited, breaking control of my limbs as the match fell, falling and falling as I frenzied for the fire extinguisher, my feet fumbling and flying up like feathers, torso twisting, limbs lowering, the flames flaring.

Eleanor flashed, and fire struck.

The fluid toppled from my fall, smearing the dirt with chemicals that, within seconds, were alight.

Cockroaches burned to a crisp, their wings singing as they attempted to escape. Somewhere, a snake's scales charred. A cicada's call was silenced.

The fire extinguisher fumbled from my fingers. Before I could clasp it, frost sprayed, surrounding Eleanor and me with a circle of snow.

Her portrait was burnt but its core kept constant.

From this she rose, paint forming the particles of her hair, her mother's words the texture of her eyes, my blood her flesh.

This skin pressed mine, its fingers falling through, but a memory of my skin as the barn burned, triggering sirens so far in the distance they seemed echoes of sounds, callings of the bull.

I brought my hand to my heart and watched without whispering while

Eleanor, Eleanor ... Eleanor

vanished.

With the wind, buried in the dust.

Purged through coughing as the barn crumbled and I realized, so, too, might I.

Blood beat and burned hotter than the flames scathing my skin. I lived and breathed and wanted to breathe and live every beat and breath I could, not die in the shadow of death.

Clutching the painting, pushing through smoke so thick in stench it rendered me senseless, I tried to trudge through the lineless labyrinth.

Beams fell before and behind, crashing beside the ash-covered canvas until, from the layers of yellow and orange and bright, the darkness of Rosewood was in sight, its silhouette so bright I stopped, marveling in the majesty of home, of death, of *mine.*

A rusting light fixture shattered.

Flames roared, and I ran, glass slicing my bare soles but barely feeling as feet pounded hot soil, driving shards deeper into my flesh as I expelled myself from flames; blood and blackness were all I recognized of the body below my head, and the painting beside it.

My insides escaped, the entries and exits of my body unable to suppress my stomach as I fell and gripped it, the seconds before she came an eternity of ecstasy and agony. My work complete, pain that would not, could not cease until her hand held my hair and tears touched my skin, her voice a melody though the words curses, calls to sirens blaring in the background, blending and burning into the blaze as bright behind me, the barn banished itself to banality, breaking over its own beams and under itself into earth.

Red and white.

Red and night, as my eyes closed, and I saw my mother's face and felt her hold me, heard her beg someone to take care of me and whisper, "Everything will be alright."

CHAPTER THIRTY-THREE

W ait, *not yet.*
    Were my first words when I woke.

How I knew the child had been born is beyond my memory, so maybe these words were not as I recall, but I did know, as though it must have been that as barn and flesh burned, the baby was birthed.

Emily's eyes told me. They were softer and sweeter than I'd ever seen, sending my heart aflutter with a thousand and one other worries, questions, and concerns. But before I could comment and commit to their cause, the last layer of our old love lay.

"The portrait."

Question, declaration, exclamation surpassing proper punctuation, and Emily's answer, acknowledgment, and affection all in one affirmation as her hands stroked singed skin, her nose nuzzling and her forehead thudding mine while her lips ever so slightly kissed.

No words need answer; the portrait was image, not poem.

And as soon as Emily's kisses were of the past, so too was the piece of art.

"It's a girl," she said and breathed life with words into the body, which I soon gave the name, "Elizabeth."

The name came as I held her, after her mother but not quite, a z in exchange for Elisabeth's s, and, as though to concede, the baby rejected the breast Sissy was reluctant to give, relishing the bottle I eagerly offered, barely leaving my arms between the hospital and Rosewood, where the portrait, partially burned and entirely complete, hung above an excess of baby gifts in the form of unwrapped online orders sent from all over the world.

My sister showed up unannounced and uninvited with a cheap gift that shrunk beside the expensive stuffed animals Lana Lane sent. Initially, I was so tired from sleepless nights that I nearly asked her to leave, but when Lizzy's fingers tugged at her hair and wouldn't let go, we laughed and the iciness between us began to thaw.

Soon, she was over often for play dates and walks around the ranch.

After one week became another, and one month, two, and nearly three, I saw what became of Sissy and me and realized what we perhaps had always been.

She was sad, perpetually, and I said I would support her, but whenever I held her or initiated sex, Lizzy's screams interrupted, and we inevitably argued. We had a baby, I insisted. There wasn't time for *us* when Lizzy needed caring for.

Sissy sneered over the nickname, claiming it was too early to call a child in partiality. "You have a baby. All I got from giving birth is post-partum depression," she spat, and as soon as she said it, we knew it was over.

She stayed through the summer and then went away to school, not to my alma mater as planned but to Emily's.

Emily drove her, and when she returned with wet eyes, I was struck by the dryness of my own irises, so I went to paint, but the bit of red I squirted from the tube began to crack after hours of sitting, so I took off the next day to Austin to drink at a college bar and make out with the first young woman I saw.

The stranger was soaking wet when I touched her, and from her shyness, I understood she'd never had done this with a woman before but was too ashamed to say so. Seeing Sissy's shuddering under her boyfriend's shadow, I tugged down the girl's underwear. I knelt in front of her, interlacing our fingers as she clasped the lock to a stall handle that wouldn't shut. I shoved my tongue inside her, licking her as her hands grasped my hair. She gasped, heaving her weight against the swinging door, my mouth moving in sync with the music I was glad blared over her moans, covering her voice so in my mind I still heard Sissy's when she came.

Pulling her panties up for her, I stood to lean my body against the door while she adjusted her clothes, and other girls came in, snickering at the sight of four feet in the stall. Her face flushed, and once the others left, she started awkwardly fingering me. I shriveled dry, seeing Lizzy fumbling around in twenty years.

I left the girl with a kiss on the forehead.

The next time I went out, it was to the sort of bar where everyone knew when to stop drinking. The woman I brought home was roughly my own age, and she didn't mind when Lizzy's crying interrupted our sex.

I went to check, but Emily was already there. I told her to go back to bed, but she was too cozy to let Lizzy go, and not wanting to leave yet, I sat by them, resting my head on Emily's shoulder and watching Lizzy struggle to finish her bottle.

"I never understood why mothers would say they want to eat their children," I said as I played with Lizzy's toes.

Emily gave some unnecessary explanation, but we knew I now knew the desire as she did and understood it just as little.

After enough time passed, Emily told me to return to bed, telling me not to let the baby interfere with my sex so I wouldn't resent her later.

So, I let the woman whose name I would forget the following day fuck me, and soon I let other women make love to me after actual dates with conversations about books and careers.

When alone, I watched my sex tape with Lana for the first time since it was leaked, and when I wasn't alone, I started looking into the eyes of the women in my bed.

I wrote Sissy some sort of apology, the style weak and cliché, the content sincere. She thanked me and promised to reply but never did, so I never bothered her.

She still held space in my soul, and in my spare time, I painted her, a single expressionist-esque piece amidst lifelike depictions of Lizzy, of Emily and Lizzy, of Rosewood and us, as though the strokes were pixels captured on a screen, only slightly altering the colors and shadows as I approached from the fields, my boots collecting dust as I adjusted the straw hat, smiling as Emily held up Lizzy's little fingers to wave and laughing when Lizzy formed foam on her lips, my heart bursting and breaking the confines of my bones as she giggled in my arms. I smelled the soft, sweet scent of baby powder and clean cloth diapers wafting effervescently of coconut.

I rubbed my nose against hers, breathing in memories of the moment I'd smelled Sissy in the grocery store, my skin tingling as I recollected the sensation of her skin brushing mine, forgiving but never forgetting the bites I'd left on her body, the bruises that remained inside, and feeling the wounds buried within my flesh that would never fade, and feeling, as Emily brushed her hands through my tangled hair, the trauma we shared, sensing the sorrow separate from mine, distinct to her yet interconnected to me, a disease that had strengthened us, had given birth to the painting and to Lizzy, to the memories of Eleanor, to the satisfaction of our skin, and to the contentment that this would never be complete, that there would eternally be turns of yearning, burning, desiring, of lacking and substituting love.

That picture seemed so perfect, so whole, that I would love to leave it there, but that would not be true, and truly, I still desire to extend that moment through time, but for this cycle, only a final circle remains, and from this Texan sunset, we remain at Rosewood.

Chapter Thirty-Four

Coming not to the end, and not to Eleanor's, nor to Sissy's nor Lizzy's, Rosewood's or Lana Lane's nor even to mine, but to a final twist as, seven years since the portrait came to its end and Lizzy's life its beginning, I wake, and go, as I do every year to the space where twice seven years ago, a part of me perished.

After the ashes and rotting wood had been cleared, dirt was laid for a pasture.

A tree would have been symbolic but stereotypical, so we introduced dairy to the ranch.

In mid-May, that meant calves were frolicking about, most soon to be veal, others to be slaughtered later in the season for young beef, one or two to be spared to make milk, and children to repeat the cycle.

Eleanor would have approved, and Emily had with her dying breath, though I doubt her last words had been a literal sanctioning of this space where she, too, came to her death.

One morning, some years since my daughter was born and Sissy grew up and went away and I'd decided to stay, Emily came to this same spot.

One of her young lovers – I'd conceded to stop calling them cowboy fucks – had been with her and later said she left without a word, still in her nightgown with a robe around her and cowgirl boots slipped over her ankles.

I found her on my jog, her chest crumpled over the fence's splinters, her heart having given out.

I've imagined many times what she said, thought, and felt in that final second. The moment became the subject of one of my finest pieces and can be seen in a gallery somewhere, maybe in Madrid or London, but probably in Vienna.

I leave Emily to imagine what those thoughts and feelings might have been so she might spend that private, final moment with Eleanor, or alone, if that's what she would prefer.

I weep for her as much as I weep for Eleanor, wallowing in grief, bringing my body to the earth as I nourish the soil with the saline of my sweat and chemicals of my cries, shedding lakes of sun-kissed skin over the dirt as the sun rises and my soul lifts from its sunken state.

The twelfth of May, 2027.

I return to Rosewood, and as I slide open the door, one of the girls squeezes past, headphones in ear as she rushes into her run.

I roll my eyes, but before I reach the kitchen, I'm yelled at.

"Kitty! You're in my shot!"

My shoulders bounce as I realize another one is sitting on the couch with a cell phone propped up facing the TV. She's creating an experimental film.

I ask if she's been up all night.

"I need to watch what I'm filming!"

Which is an unchanging blank screen. "I don't care, Annie; it's—" I stop, swearing as I realize my mistake and wish Lana hadn't named her daughters Annie, Aria, and Angela.

"Stop acting like my mom when you can't remember my name!"

"I am your mom," Lana interrupts as she comes down the stairs and adjusts her recently re-dyed hair. "And I mix up your names all the time. And Kitty's right. It is a school night."

"That's why I slept in my uniform! So I wouldn't waste time getting ready."

"That's disgusting. Go change." Angela pouts, but Lana points upstairs and gives her a look that makes me squirm. "Especially your socks!" she calls over her shoulder, but as soon as the door slams, she looks at me, and we are the only ones in the world.

After wrinkles and teeth whitening, screaming children and stupid arguments, funerals, and fresh starts, the earth still stills on its axis as her eyes fix as my center, her skin enclosing the cosmos of my heart, my embrace becoming the skeleton for her soul melting into mine.

"I love you," she says when there's no need except that this can't be said enough, so I say it back before kissing her. If only I could forever, but I'm thirty-nine, on the edge of middle age, and Lana is fifty-two, and two teenagers and a seven-year-old need breakfast, and we haven't had coffee.

The machine is the same one from Emily's time, and since we have dairy cows and Lana is no longer vegan, I make the cappuccinos as she fixes eggs. I haven't persuaded her to eat meat, so there is no bacon, but the sizzling still sounds like it did when Emily had lived.

"How are you today?" she asks the question more than those words.

Today how I am coping with Eleanor's death and my daughter's growth, with owning Rosewood, being with a famous actress, and being an artist.

"I cried," I admit.

"I'm sorry."

"I'm not," I say as I sip my coffee. We tell our daughters it's alright to cry, but when either of us does, we act as though it is wrong.

Lana looks up from the eggs. "Sissy called. I said you'd call her back later."

Sissy, whose name had once sent my heart skipping beats, who had reminded me to love, whose body had carried and birthed the child for whom I cared as though she came from my womb, whose name now slowed my heart into sore remorse that when in the throes of post-partum pain, she abandoned her daughter whom I protected instead of helping her, remorse that Sissy's life was more lost than mine had been when I'd met her, that instead of art she turned to drugs and existed on edges that made me dizzy to think of and remorse that our love had descended into a custody case and accusations of sexual manipulation, some of which I concede are not unfounded.

No relationship is perfect, and if I'd known how much I was hurting her, I wouldn't have behaved as I had.

Her accusations, which nearly ruined my career, left out the fact that I sent her money every month even though we never spoke and that I'd saved her from abuse.

"I'll call her later," I say, avoiding Lana's eyes.

We can talk about anything but choose not to about this.

She reaches over without glancing up from the eggs, wrapping her hand around the back of my neck as she tugs me towards her for a kiss.

I stay close, whispering, "You know I think it's sexy you can cook one-handed and kiss me at the same time."

"I could do more than kiss you."

She clicks off the burner so she can use both hands, one to hold my body and another to touch me.

I cling to her, my breaths shortening as her touch quickens and the burning inside escalates, nearly coming before shouts stop us.

"Mom! That's disgusting!"

It's Aria back from her run.

Lana stops but doesn't pull away, adjusting my shirt and underwear for me. "There's nothing disgusting about love," she tells her daughter.

Her two younger daughters like me just enough to live here. Still, even though they're old enough not to blame me for the sex tape, they remember that it ruined their Polaroid-perfect family, and the oldest daughter, away pursuing an academic career under a pseudonym, has never forgiven either of us.

"I know, but I eat in this kitchen," Aria complains, pulling out a plate.

Lana smooths the girl's sweaty hair. "Darling, why don't you shower before eating?"

"Why don't you wash your hands after finger fucking Kitty?"

"If I'd talked to my mother the way you talk to me, she would have washed my mouth with soap."

"You're making that up."

Lana laughs as she lathers her hands with soap. It's true, but she won't admit it, so I support her as I sip my lukewarm coffee. "Mine did."

The girl backfires. "We all know your childhood and life have sucked, Kitty. We're sick of hearing about it."

Lana glares, looking as though she could hit her. "Aria Valerie Ray, do you realize how insensitive that is? Today of all days?"

Aria's flushed face pales.

"It's alright," I say before she apologizes, setting my coffee cup in the sink before kissing Lana. "I'll go wake Lizzy."

At the stairs, Angela rushes past in a clean uniform without looking up from the screen in her hand. Lana and Aria's voices escalate, but I block them out as I pass the finger painting from when I was five.

Across from it hangs one Lizzy painted at the same age.

After inheriting the estate, I donated the collector's pieces to museums. Now the only famous works in Rosewood are mine and the acting awards Lana hides in our sex drawer.

Rosewood is no longer the antler-decked ranch Eleanor and I ran around in, nor is it the sleek, artsy mansion Sissy and I fell in love in.

The door to Lizzy's room is decorated with pink, glittery letters and a hand-drawn picture of rainbows and unicorns so stereotypically feminine that they mock my gender-neutral parenting.

The lights are off, curtains drawn. A seascape hums by the bed.

Her cowgirl doll has fallen, so I lean down to pick it up, lying next to her as I set the doll on the other side of the pillow.

Snuggling close, I rest a hand over the light brown chair I suspect comes from her father. I've never seen a photograph of him, but Sissy's hair is dark, unyielding. In contrast, Lizzy's smoothens to my will when I brush it, and Lizzy's eyes are Sissy's. Still, her movements are mine, her phrases sometimes Lana's, and occasionally Emily sneaks out.

The girl's meticulous organization reminds me of Eleanor, except Lizzy is kind and never needy, shyly blending into the background of Rosewood's strong women.

Her affection is reserved. Still, she clings to me everywhere, scribbling quietly in a notebook in which she collects words she likes. Before words, it was a notebook of letters, and before she could form those, it was a collection of colors.

On the top of every page is the word love, written differently every time, each letter a different color, and sometimes the lines of a single letter are marked in different inks. After *love* comes *picture*. Before *pony* comes *Mommy*, though, when she's mad at me, the names of her cowgirl doll's name, *Sydney*, and *Mommy* are written on the same line to have equal standing.

Closing my eyes, I bring my head near hers, breathing the smell of honeydew soap.

Lana bathed her last night. Lana is more entertaining at bath time. At everything, actually, and Lana always uses melon scents, which Lizzy likes better than my coconut and creamy spice, which I hate to tell her are what her mother liked. Lana scrubs behind Lizzy's ears better than I do, so her skin is soft and delicate, even flaky under my lips.

She will wake soon, rub her eyes, and curl into a little ball while she squeezes her eyes, pretending to still be sleeping. But she won't fight about waking up. Not when I remind her it's her birthday.

But her body is so still her dreams must be sweet, so I stay for as many seconds as I can with my hand around her body, her belly rising as evenly as the sound of the waves over the sand or a steady breeze that is not yet wind, and in these seconds, and in the seconds in-between, I am satisfied.

ABOUT THE AUTHOR

Katherine Dahlquist-Bauer is a Texan-Austrian writer, photographer, and artist.

As the host of the bilingual radio show Film Fatal, she explores the role of women in the film industry. She has also written travel pieces, free prose, and screenplays.

This is her debut novel.

She can be found digitally on social media as @cosmopolitankat. In the physical world, she might be more difficult to track down.

Made in the USA
Monee, IL
07 August 2024

63435286R10136